THE RAVEN

Clan Ross of Skye

The Raven: Clan Ross of Skye
USA Today Bestselling Author
Hildie McQueen

Copyright © 2024 by Hildie McQueen
Print Edition

All rights reserved. No part of this book may be reproduced in any form or by any electronic or mechanical means—except in the case of brief quotations embodied in critical articles or reviews—without written permission.

The characters and events portrayed in this book are fictitious. Any similarity to real persons, living or dead, is purely coincidental and not intended by the author.

Also By Hildie McQueen

Clan Ross of Skye
The Wolf
The Hawk
The Raven
The Falcon

Clan Ross of the Hebrides
The Lion: Darach
The Beast: Duncan
The Eagle: Stuart
The Fox: Caelan
The Stag: Artair
The Duke: Clan Ross Prequel
The Bear: Cynden

Clan Ross Series
A Heartless Laird
A Hardened Warrior
A Hellish Highlander
A Flawed Scotsman
A Fearless Rebel
A Fierce Archer

Moriag Series
Beauty and the Highlander
The Lass and the Laird
Lady and the Scot
The Laird's Daughter

Note From the Author

I am often asked why I usually portray my characters of color as mixed ethnicities. It is mainly because being multi-racial myself, I can easily relate to a person who has more than one ethnicity.

I am portraying the heroine, Nala Maclaren, as Afro-Scottish. Her mother is of Afro-Caribbean descent. Her father is full Scottish.

Africans and Caribbeans began arriving in the UK in the late 1400s, some brought as servants, others as entertainers. It is well known that a pair of African sisters and an African man were part of King James' court.

The identity of Black Scottish people has evolved since the arrival of black people in Scotland as early as the 15th century, with significant numbers arriving in the 20th century after World War II. The development of a cohesive Black Scottish identity has progressed, with Black African and Afro-Caribbean descent being the most commonly claimed ancestry.

Hildie McQueen

CHAPTER ONE

Heaviness, like a sodden cloak, weighed over him as Alexander Ross rode away from the small cottage on his lands.

His visit had been met with tears of sorrow and a lack of hope. Months had passed since the brutal and senseless murder of the man who'd been the lifeline of the grief-stricken family and still, he, their laird, had not been able to find the killers.

Alexander Ross gave in to the futility of the situation, allowing the exhaustion and despair he kept well-hidden when around others. It was imperative that as laird, he seemed unshakable. Unstoppable. And most importantly that he could always maintain control of his emotions.

For the most part, he'd succeeded. Only a few times had the curtain fallen, but only around those closest to him. It was when in the presence of his brothers and cousin, that he'd confided the frustration of not being able to capture the group of men who terrorized Clan Ross.

A roar of frustration fought to surface, but Alexander kept it restrained. How much longer before his people would witness the defeat of the heartless group of men who, up to this point, had managed to kill clans' people and evade being caught? They could not hide forever. Something or someone would eventually have to give them up. Everyone had a price, something they would willingly exchange for information.

Alexander had little doubt that he and his men would find the cowards. The only obstacles were time and patience, neither of which he had an abundance of. Already talk of his lack of ability to keep the clan's people safe was spreading across the villages and farmlands.

Fear rushed through his lands like a river overrunning its banks. Understandably, the people were scared and unfortunately that fear could lead to unrest.

There was nothing worse than a clan living in fear. People would become suspicious of their neighbors, see enemies where none existed, and eventually their suspicions could cause them to turn against one another. Once that happened, it would take an act of God to bring order back to the land.

His surroundings became eerily silent; the only sound was the wind rustling through leaves. Years of training alerted him that something was amiss. Just then the snap of branches told him a presence was nearby.

Alexander pulled his horse to a stop and stilled his breathing as he strained to listen. He needed to know what direction the sounds had come from.

The murmur of men's voices came from his left, so he slowly pulled back on the reins of his horse, forcing the animal to walk backward into some high bushes. He and the steed were not fully hidden, as most of his body remained above the foliage, but hopefully it was enough for someone passing in the distance to not take notice of him.

Alexander leaned forward, narrowing his eyes in an attempt to see through the trees. Finally there was movement.

Whoever they were, they rode a short distance away. He allowed his breath to release because unless the men were alerted, they would not notice him.

First one, then a second, then finally two more came into view. With each one, his heart hammered harder, faster. Could it be them? The attackers?

They were certainly not familiar.

Barely able to keep still, he waited until it was safe to urge his mount forward to follow them. Soon they would leave the safety of the forest, and he would be exposed; so he would have to follow at a distance. For the moment, he kept them as close as he dared, hoping to figure out where their hiding place was.

When the men hesitated, seeming to stop to have a discussion, Alexander moved behind a pair of trees. He peered around just as one of the men turned to scan the area. He ducked back behind the tree praying the low foliage disguised his mount. The beast was a dark brown, almost black, which helped camouflage it among the dark tree trunks and shrubbery. However, a keen eye would be able to notice it.

The air stilled, barely rustling the leaves surrounding him and Alexander cursed under his breath. The movement of branches and leaves helped take attention from anything that moved. He took a quick look to his horse, praying the proud animal wasn't swooshing its full tail. Thankfully, the beast seemed to understand the silent command to be still.

As slowly as possible, Alexander glanced around the tree again. The men had moved. They were not where he'd last seen them. Two remained, their mounts still, both looking in his direction.

He'd been discovered.

Alexander yanked up on his mounts' reins, willing the horse to turn back in the direction he'd come, just as the other two men appeared. One to his right, the other to his left.

Alexander reached for the sword tucked in the scabbard on his back.

"I would nae try to fight us, warrior," one of the men said. His eyes narrowed and lips curled in distaste. "Or should I say, Ross?"

A quick assessment confirmed the only way to escape would be to take the men down, it meant, however, that he'd have his back to the other two. Alexander weighed his options. He'd fought more than one man at a time before. Despite being laird, he'd gone to battle many times, before and after his father's death.

Being outnumbered was not new to him, nor was it frightening. What was worrisome, was that the other two had neared, therefore doubling the number of men he'd have to fight and beat if he had any hope of escaping alive.

The odds were definitely against him. It was a fleeting thought that he ignored.

He was a seasoned warrior, one with an elevated ego, therefore he pushed away any thoughts of defeat. Assessing each man carefully, he realized only two had the flat look of a warrior. The other two lost the battle of meeting his gaze when he locked eyes with them.

"Are ye who have attacked my people?" Alexander's voice was strong and even, making the weak pair exchange looks of surprise.

Their silence answered his question.

"Today ye will die, Ross," said one of the men he recognized as a warrior. Perhaps he'd even fought him in the past. If Alexander were to guess, he was the self-appointed leader of the group.

Witnesses had claimed to have seen a band of six men. If four of them were here, it meant they'd either lost the other two or, for whatever reason, they did not accompany them on that day.

It occurred to him the men had recognized him as one of the Ross brothers, but not as laird. Alexander wasn't sure if it was to his advantage or not. Finally, he decided it didn't matter. If he divulged who he was, they would either take glee in killing him or feel forced to kill him as he'd seen their faces and could recognize them.

"Whether it be all of ye at once, or one at a time, it will be each of ye who will die for what ye've done." Once again, the weaker duo exchanged worried glances.

"Strong words for someone outnumbered," the one who'd last spoken said. He spat on the ground. He eyed Alexander's sword as if assessing how to attack.

"Not used to attacking someone who is prepared?" Alexander chided. "Is it only as a group that ye can expect to beat and kill innocent unarmed people?" He huffed and looked up to the sky. "A defenseless chicken farmer or a lone young guard. It does nae say much about yer abilities."

The spokesman of the group growled. "I can down ye by myself. I dinnae need help."

This time the other three looked to one another in question. The man who'd spoken addressed them. "I will kill him. Dinnae feel as if ye need to assist me."

By the long look he gave the others, they were to remain at

a distance unless the man motioned for them, which Alexander suspected he would eventually.

Alexander was a formidable opponent, his horse trained to fight another horse. Something that often caught his enemies by surprise.

With a wild cry, the man charged toward him, which was ridiculous given the fact he was surrounded by foliage and meant his horse had to slow down to make its way forward.

As soon as the attacker neared, Alexander swung his sword, taking advantage of the charging man's lack of balance. The blade flew across the man's side slicing into his arm. It was not a deep cut, but enough to draw blood.

The trio of idiots inched forward, but his opponent held a hand up. He snarled in Alexander's direction, lifting his sword, bringing it down and across. Alexander easily blocked, pushed back, and jabbed his weapon forward. The man had battle experience as he managed to lean away, swinging his steed to avoid being impaled.

Twice again their swords clanged, the sound of metal against metal vibrating through the trees. The men had awkwardly encircled them due to the low-growing bushes and plants.

The horses lifted their legs as they traversed the uneven terrain, nostrils flared, grunting as they expelled sharp breaths. The animals were war horses, accustomed to being handled not only as transport but also as weapons and shields.

Alexander turned his horse the opposite direction of where his opponent moved, catching the man off guard, then with his right foot he tapped his steed's hind right leg. The animal understood the command and kicked out both legs, hitting the hindquarters of the other man's horse before moving away.

Surprised, his opponent's horse did what came naturally. It reared up, bucked, and kicked its legs as a reflex. The man atop the horse momentarily lost his balance giving Alexander the prime opportunity to thrust his sword into his side.

The man let out a howl of pain, then kicked his steed to move away from Alexander.

Not waiting for a signal, the other three advanced.

Alexander held his sword up with both hands facing them. From the way the injured man was panting and leaning forward over his horse, both hands clasped to where he bled, he was no longer a threat.

"This is nae the first time I've faced four men. As ye can see I still live," Alexander stated. The men hesitated just long enough for him to gather some strength and calm his breathing.

Suddenly as one, with a combination of grunts and battle cries, the attackers advanced.

Just as quickly one of them screamed and fell from his mount, with an arrow impaled through his neck. The other two pulled back on their horses searching the area.

Unsure what to think, Alexander didn't dare look around. He still had two opponents. Three if he counted the man he'd injured, who moved closer to the other two and seemed to be sitting straighter in the saddle.

"Withdraw." The injured man's voice was low as he spoke, the entire time glaring at Alexander. The injured man was surrounded by the others and then the three men galloped away.

Moving back behind trees, he studied the surroundings.

Where was the archer?

He considered giving chase but thought better of it. He'd been lucky that only one had fought him. He wasn't about to press his luck and try to fight three.

However, it was imperative he find out where they hid, he considered waiting and then following them.

"I would nae go after them," a feminine voice stated. "Injured dogs are dangerous."

A lone woman emerged from behind a tree. Dressed in dark green breeches and matching tunic, she held a longbow in one hand and the reins to a beautiful gray gelding in the other.

She was not tall, but neither was the lass slight. There was a sense of assurance about her as she walked with even steps, her shoulders back, and an impassive expression. Her skin was a rare color of golden autumn leaves, her eyes a beautiful sunset brown, and her lips were plump, the kind that most men would kill to taste.

As she walked closer, her gaze moved over him. "Ye dinnae look to be injured."

The breeze blew a strand of hair across her face, and she brushed it away. Her light brown thick lush curls were pulled back into a single braid down her back. Some tendrils had managed to get free framing the most beautiful face he'd ever seen.

Something about her was very familiar. Her eyes, the shape of her face. The thick lush hair.

Perhaps she was related to someone he knew.

The picture of a young lass he'd known a long time past formed. She'd been perhaps ten and two and had often followed Alexander and his brothers about when they'd played in the woods.

Could it be?

She'd finally come close enough that he could reach out and touch her. Her almond-shaped eyes met his, a playful smile teasing the edges of her luscious lips.

It had to be the wee lass, now fully grown. No longer the cute wee girl he remembered, but a vision that made his mouth go dry.

"Na-Nala?" Alexander stuttered. "Is it ye?"

CHAPTER TWO

NALA SCANNED THE surroundings to ensure the men had not doubled back. Instead of doing the same, Alexander's gaze remained focused on her.

"Who were those men?" she asked, not answering his question.

He gave her a searching look before turning his attention to the direction the men had gone. "Could be Mackinnons."

His attention wasn't diverted for long, once again his deep green eyes returned to her. "Nala, ye've returned."

Obviously he wouldn't be deterred from what he wanted to know. Unable to keep from it, she smiled. "Aye. I have returned from my banishment. My parents could nae keep me tucked away in England any longer."

For a long moment he said nothing, his broad chest continuing to lift and lower from having fought.

It had been over ten years since she'd last seen Alexander and he'd changed a great deal. Gone was the handsome young man who allowed her and his younger brothers to trail behind. In his place now stood a man.

Needing to keep from gawking, she glanced over her shoulder. "I remember following ye and yer brothers through this portion of the forest."

Alexander walked toward her. "Aye, ye insisted I teach ye

to hunt whenever I took Cynden out." Once again he studied her. "Why were ye gone so long?" The closer he walked, the more she noticed the changes in him.

His shoulders were broader, his jawline stronger, and his eyes... there was something different about them. Once so expressive you could easily know his emotions and what he thought. Now, they were flat—devoid of any emotion.

Nala let out a long breath and looked away from his face, suddenly feeling awkward in his presence. "I was sent to live with Father's sister in London. My parents had hopes that I would learn to be a highborn lady and find a suitable husband."

When Alexander remained silent, yet seemed interested, Nala continued, "For years I attended balls and fetes, it was the most boring existence I could imagine. I had to find a distraction from the constant matchmaking and frilly frocks, which meant I learned the skill of hiding in plain sight."

The corners of his lips twitched. "Most women like that sort of thing. Do they nae?"

Nala shrugged. "I'd prefer to gouge my eyes out with a dirk than to stand about in hot ballrooms with a glass of tepid punch."

"So I take it by hiding and such, it helped pass the time?"

"That and I found a way to fill the long stretches of time I was expected to sit about and sew or read. I hired an expert to teach me the sword and another to assist in honing my archery skills." She grinned. "Much better use of time."

"I take it ye were found out?" Alexander asked.

Nala nodded. "Aye, my aunt happened upon me dressed in men's clothing whilst engaged in sword practice. She wrote my parents, and they insisted it was time I return to Skye."

She couldn't help smiling at the memory of her aunt's expression when she'd caught her during sword fighting lessons behind the stables.

Once again, the corners of his mouth twitched into what she suspected was as much of a smile as he was going to give her. "I am glad that ye returned. England is no place for a Scottish lass."

He looked past her into the woods and scowled. "Nala, no matter yer skills, it is dangerous for ye to be about alone in the forest. It is nae safe as of late."

"I noticed," Nala quipped.

"I will ride with ye to yer home." Alexander mounted not waiting to see if she followed suit.

She'd just saved him and now he thought she required protection. Although she wanted to laugh, Nala looked up to him with mock innocence. "I assure you, I am more than capable of returning home without an escort. Ye should see about returning to the keep."

Alexander's eyes narrowed as he waited for her to mount.

Perhaps it was better to do as he said. It would keep him from going to her father and telling him how she was in the forest and not at her friend's home as she'd said.

She mounted and looked to Alexander, who looked every bit a highlander atop his steed. His blue-black shoulder-length hair, trimmed beard, and deep emerald green eyes came together to form a beautiful man. In a dark tunic and matching breeches that were tucked into sturdy boots, he was dressed for riding. The sword was now sheathed into the scabbard strapped to his wide back and next to his right leg strapped to the saddle was another broadsword.

"If ye have somewhere to be, I can see myself home. No need to delay yer travels any further," Nala said. Mainly because she didn't wish for him to see her parents and tell them where she'd been.

Alexander brought his mount alongside, his gaze constantly scanning the surroundings and landing on her from time to time. "Come to the keep with yer parents. I am sure Mother would be happy to see ye."

Nala wondered why he'd not mentioned his father and made a mental note to ask her parents about it. Perhaps the laird had fallen ill or was gone somewhere.

They came to a fork in the road, one side leading to Keep Ross, the other to her father's lands. Nala lifted a hand. "I will ensure my parents are informed of yer invitation. There is little doubt that they will gladly accept."

"Yer mother and mine remain good friends," Alexander informed her. "I am surprised my mother didnae ken of yer return."

Nala considered the information. "Perhaps she does ken but has nae told ye."

Alexander acquiesced with a shrug.

A fortnight had passed since her return, and her mother had lectured her nonstop about her actions in England, informing her that her lack of propriety had embarrassed the family. Although a kind and gentle woman, her mother was determined that Nala should marry soon. Stating again and again that at Nala's age, most women were not only married but had several bairns. Nala wasn't sure if it was true or not, but from what she noted on the surrounding lands, it seemed probable.

If she'd not informed Alexander's mother of her return, it was probably because she'd not come up with an explanation as to why, after spending her marriageable years in London, Nala remained unmarried.

She wondered if her mother still held on to the dream of Nala marrying a Ross. Of course that was not to be, now that all of Alexander's brothers were married.

The only one not married was Alexander, who was in line to be laird. He would probably marry someone who would be beneficial for the clan. A marriage brokered by his parents. Alexander would have little say in who he married. So he was never to be her husband.

Nala slid a look at him. He was certainly handsome and perhaps of good nature. At least, from what she remembered, he'd been even-tempered, patient, and kind. But he had always been a somber man, one who took things seriously.

It was for the best that he and she could not marry. From his actions that day, he would insist she remain in the safety of the keep and not out riding, which she enjoyed. It was understandable of course, as the wife of a future laird, there was always the danger of being taken and leaving their children orphaned.

Seeming to sense her regard, Alexander turned to her, and Nala quickly looked away.

"I find it strange that ye are allowed out alone," Alexander said. "That yer husband or betrothed allows it."

Since it wasn't a question, Nala shrugged and didn't speak. She'd thought to have made it clear to not have found either in England. But if he wanted to make assumptions, who was she to take it away from him.

The fact that there were few eligible men on Skye who would be approved by her mother and father was fortunate as Nala had no intentions of marrying. A life with her parents in their beautiful home surrounded by plush lands was not a bad way to live.

In England, she found fault with every suitor—not that there were many—as she was considered a Scottish wilding by the elite circle her aunt and uncle surrounded themselves with. Not just that, but the thought of remaining in England, away from her family and home was another reason she'd not accepted the few offers that had been proffered.

Her aunt became frustrated when all her matchmaking efforts brought no results, until she ultimately gave up.

They continued toward her home and Nala still hoped that Alexander would leave her and go in the direction of the keep. She didn't want to take a chance that her father would see him and ask questions about how far she'd ridden.

Unfortunately, he continued to ride beside her and after studying her for a long moment he said, "Ye have changed."

Nala took the moment to take him in. Gone was the young man she'd known. He'd been replaced by a formidable warrior. Waves of raven black hair now fell to his shoulders, and his piercing eyes seemed a darker shade of green. His face no longer soft from youth, instead now chiseled into what she could only describe as perfection. He was a study in beauty.

"I am now two and twenty. Have been away for years. Of course, I have changed." She gave him a pointed look. "I can say the same about ye."

He slid a look toward her probably expecting her to say

more. When she didn't his gaze bore into hers. "Why does yer husband allow ye free rein to go about alone?" This time his tone was stern.

Of course she wasn't allowed to ride out alone. If her father found out she'd gone as far as the forest, he'd be furious with her. Alexander didn't have to know that fact. Despite the dangers, she felt competent to go for short rides and protect herself. She was not a weakling.

She took a deep breath in an effort to keep her temper in check. Of course Alexander had every right to be concerned at seeing her out alone. Seemed some of her training in England had indeed taken root. "I am nae married. Nor do I ever wish to be," she quickly added. "That I go for short rides near my home should nae be anyone's concern."

When Alexander cleared his throat, she narrowed her eyes. "And before ye say another word ken that Father allows me to ride, as long as I stay nearby, but I am nae a person to be kept *reined in*", she said emphasizing the last two words.

He nodded. "Understood. But I will say that even my warriors dinnae ride out alone these days. I am nae allowing my men to. I am nae only saying it because ye are a woman. That bow and arrow cannae help against six men if they were to attack ye."

His words mollified her. "Father did mention about the attacks. So far they'd been away from our lands." She looked over toward the trees. "Why did they attack ye?"

"They must have recognized me. It would be a triumph to their cause if they were to kill the laird."

Laird.

Nala whirled to face him, sure her expression was incredulous. "Ye are laird now?"

His shoulders lifted and lowered as if it were nothing of importance. "Aye, two years now."

Memories of his father flooded her mind. The late laird had been formidable and yet kind with her when she'd been a wee bairn. Once, when she'd fallen and skinned her knees, he'd lifted her into his arms to console her and then carried her into the house to be given sweets.

"Wh-what happened to him?" Tears welled up and Nala did her best to blink them away. Turning her head, she wiped away an errant tear that trailed down her face.

"I was nae aware ye didnae ken," Alexander stated. "Did yer mother nae write ye about it?"

Nala shook her head, tears now flowing freely down her cheeks. "She kept bad news from me out of fear I would insist on returning." Her voice trembled. "I loved yer father. What happened?"

It occurred to her too late that the question would be hurtful to Alexander. "Ye dinnae have to answer. I am shocked that is all."

"Wounded in battle with the Mackinnons," he said in a soft voice. "The wounds festered."

Nala sniffed picturing the proud man suffering. "Can we stop for a moment?" Not waiting for a reply, she pulled the horse to a stop and dismounted. She walked a few steps away hoping for privacy as grief overtook her.

Bowing her head, she covered her face with both hands and let out a soft sob. The last thing she wanted was to cry in front of Alexander and bring him pain, but it couldn't be helped. She truly loved the late laird; he was like an uncle to her. Pain tightened in her chest as she allowed herself to cry.

Blowing out a breath, she looked upwards to the cloudless sky willing the tears away. Taking several breaths until the urge to cry began to ebb. She would have to grieve later, for now she had to return home.

Nala sensed his presence before turning to look at him. Alexander stood just a bit behind her looking past her, straight ahead, jaw tight. "He was a good man. I can only aspire to one day be like him."

"He was," Nala replied. "If only I'd returned for a visit and seen him."

They were silent for a few moments, Alexander seeming to sense she required time to regain control of her emotion.

"We should get ye home. I have much to do upon returning to the keep," he said.

Somehow she knew that to tell him he should go straight home and not accompany her was useless, so instead, Nala hurried to her horse. "Let us ride at a faster pace, so ye can get home sooner. As laird, ye must have many duties requiring yer attention."

They galloped the rest of the way. When her home came into view, Alexander turned his horse away. He didn't say anything, only waved.

Nala slowed her horse and watched as Alexander disappeared past the hills. She wondered what would happen upon his arrival. In all probability, he'd gather men, and they would return to the area of the attack. The task of tracking the men would be easy because one of them was bleeding and would leave a trail.

As much as she hated that the men had gotten away before

she'd been able to shoot another one, she wouldn't risk going back and being caught. That would be foolish.

She was very good at hiding, but it was still a risk. That day she'd not planned to do more than practice all she had learned in London. Using the tactics her tutor had taught her in the art of blending into the background, she continued to practice hoping to hone her skills.

Her lips curved at remembering people walking or riding past as she stood mere steps away. Her abilities would prove useful because she had plans that would test her sword and archery skills.

THE NEXT DAY was rather gloomy. Gray clouds overhead with light rain falling, which was perfect for her to hide effectively, so she planned to continue her training. Instead of staying on the ground, she would climb a tree and keep vigil. Hopefully, people would come around and give her an idea of whether or not her concealment worked.

Trained to stand and wait untethered, her horse, Shadow, kept still, his eyes on her as she bent at the waist and hurried toward a tree. Dressed from her head to her feet in dark green helped with blending into her surroundings. Her hair was a light shade of brown, which she braided and tucked underneath a knitted cap. Instead of wearing what would be considered appropriate for a woman, Nala wore a skirt that split down the center and was sewn in half.

When she stood, it was hard to tell her skirts split like breeches. Handy as her mother would immediately send her to change. Nala had purchased several additional skirts before leaving England as she'd often worn them when training with her tutor.

She looked in the direction of her home feeling a bit guilty about having lied and told her mother she was riding to visit Sencha, who lived just over the ridge, a short ride from home. She would go to Sencha's after leaving the woods. She only planned to remain there long enough for someone to ride past.

Settling in the crook of a branch, she lifted her bow and waited. From where she sat it was possible to see quite a distance and soon a wagon came into view. A man and woman sat on the bench; the back of the wagon was loaded with sacks.

Nala shifted and waited for them to near. She would throw down a few small rocks to catch their attention and wait to see if they saw her.

Closer and closer, the pair continued. Nala settled onto the branch relaxing her body to keep from stiffening as it would be a while before they were close enough.

A trio of riders came into view, but they were too far for her to see their features. The hairs on her nape rose at the thought it could be the aggressors. It was improbable, Nala told herself. Alexander had badly injured one of the men who'd attacked him, and she'd shot another. Surely the injured man would not be up to riding again so soon.

From her vantage point, she could see that the men were riding straight for the oblivious couple.

Nala notched an arrow and waited, all the while praying the men continued past the wagon without incident.

The wagon continued in her direction and Nala noted the horsemen had picked up speed. Her heart thundered at the thought of the couple being assaulted. Breathing even, she looked down to see what her horse did. The animal remained where she'd left him, bent down nibbling grasses. Good. He wouldn't be visible from the road.

Once again, she tracked the wagon. The man must have noticed the riders because he urged the horse to go faster. It wouldn't do any good, their horse was no match for the unencumbered ones that galloped toward them until finally surrounding the wagon so that they had to come to a stop.

The men circled the wagon, swords drawn. One of them must have said something because the driver of the wagon shook his head and motioned with both hands to his companion. Then he pulled the woman behind him, in a futile attempt to shield her.

Nala's breath caught and she looked around praying to see Ross warriors coming to help.

By now the woman had begun screaming words Nala could not make out, especially as her heart was hammering so hard it echoed in her ears.

The rider closest to the wagon lifted his sword and immediately without thought, Nala loosed the arrow. It penetrated the man's right lower side, and he yelped in pain, dropping his sword.

At once the other men turned to look toward the trees. None of them looked up. Nala remained still as a statue, her breathing even, eyes locked on them.

One of the attackers moved to the opposite side of the wagon to use the hapless couple as a shield.

The others continued circling their gazes searching the forest seeming at a loss as to what to do next.

When they began searching the trees, Nala leaned behind the tree, keeping her balance by tightening her thighs around the branch. With practiced efficiency, she notched a second arrow and turned back to see what happened.

One of the assailants had climbed onto the wagon and grabbed the woman, who fought against him until she lost her balance and tumbled from the wagon to the ground.

The horse harnessed to the wagon became nervous and shifted causing the attacker to struggle to remain upright. Nala took the opportunity to loose a second arrow, not bothering to see if the arrow hit where she intended but satisfied at hearing a scream of pain.

When she looked again, he'd fallen to the ground.

The aggressor with the injured side must have picked up his sword because he now held the tip of his sword at the man's chest.

"Whoever ye are, come out or I will kill him," he yelled toward the trees somehow managing to keep his horse close to the wagon whilst holding his side with one hand and the sword with the other.

Notching the third arrow, she aimed for the other man on horseback. Unfortunately, the arrow flew past his shoulder barely nicking the skin.

Nala ducked behind the tree and notched yet another arrow. But when she leaned around the tree to take aim, the two cowards were galloping away making it hard to get a clear shot because of the foliage.

Instead, she aimed for the one still on the ground. She waited until he managed to mount his horse then shot again, this time the arrow piercing the man's chest. His lifeless body fell to the ground. Nala bit her lip, keeping a sob from erupting.

She gulped and fought for breath as she kept vigil over the people on the road.

The woman hurried to her husband crying loudly her husband comforting her while looking toward the trees searching for whomever their rescuer was.

It was then her stomach tumbled and tears threatened, the thudding of her heart seeming to beat harder, pounding against her breast. She kept from looking at the dead man, instead concentrating on keeping her breathing even. The surroundings seemed to whirl around her as thoughts of what she'd done penetrated every part of her being.

A life. She'd taken a life. The thought didn't seem real. What had occurred was like a dream, a reality Nala never thought to be part of. The men meant to kill the couple, to make them pay for whatever their cause was. Still knowing she'd saved their lives didn't diminish the reality of what she'd done.

Her stomach tightened and she quickly tied the bow to the belt around her waist. Scrambling from the tree, Nala hurriedly bent over and retched, emptying the contents of her stomach. Why had she shot him again? She could have left him injured.

The tree bark was rough against her palm as she reached for it to help her remain upright. What was done was done. There was no reversing it. Tears sprung then, flowing down her face in a steady stream.

With shaky hands, Nala used water from her wineskin to wash her hands and face and then finding her horse where she'd left it, mounted and rode toward Sencha's house.

A question repeated in her mind over and over again. Was she as terrible a person as the men who'd attacked Alexander and the couple?

CHAPTER THREE

A GROUP OF people were gathered on the opposite side of the woods from where Alexander had been attacked the day before. Alexander looked over to his cousin, Knox, noting the archer's angry expression. By the way Knox gripped the horse's reins tight in his fist and scowled, he barely kept control of his fury.

On the ground, a man and woman were surrounded by several people. A messenger had come to the keep informing them that a couple had been attacked.

Everyone's attention turned to him as Alexander neared, most of them stepping over the man who lay dead near the edge of the trees.

Dismounting, he and Knox walked to the couple. "Are either of ye harmed?"

The man shook his head. "No, we are nae," he replied looking to the woman who clung to him. "They came from nowhere, approached, and said we were to die." The man continued to calmly describe all that had occurred, from the trio of men coming upon them with swords drawn to an archer saving their lives.

Immediately, Alexander wondered if once again Nala had been lurking in the woods and had been the one to save the couple from demise.

He pushed the thoughts away; the lass wouldn't be so foolish to do it again. The day she'd happened upon him, she'd claimed to be out practicing her archery, and yet, he considered it could have been a lie.

Alexander assured the couple he would do what he could to see to it the men were caught and punished. Silently, he scanned the area wondering why the attackers had come to yet another part of Ross lands.

"Do ye think it is the same men?" Knox asked him.

Alexander shook his head. "It is possible. Although two men were injured who attacked me. It has been reported many times that groups of at least six men ride together. It is surprising that once again they are in the same place."

Knox shook his head. "If they are a group large enough to split in two, why not attack as a whole?"

"Because they have no battle knowledge. Are nae prepared, instead attack as they see fit without thinking," Alexander surmised.

It was well known that Clan Ross guards patrolled in groups of four. If these men numbered eight or more, why not take on the guards?

Seeming to read his thoughts, Knox shook his head. "They attack randomly because they'd rather cause discord between ye and the people. How better than for innocents to die and the people begin to believe more and more that ye failed to protect them."

Alexander nodded. "It is what I think as well."

Upon them nearing the small group that had gathered, the people's feelings were obvious. With either looks of disappointment or open dislike, they barely acknowledged his presence. Some turned to walk a short distance away, yet unable to leave because of curiosity, while others gave barely perceptive nods of greeting. It was definitely a cool reception of their laird.

The dead man was not one of the men who'd attacked him. Alexander lowered to get a better look, studying the slight man. It was evident to him that the man had not been a warrior. Two arrows protruded from his body, one on the lower right side and one through his chest.

A man neared and handed Knox a sword. "It belonged to him, I suppose."

"No emblem," Knox observed looking to Alexander. "We ken these men are nae Clan Ross, there is only one other clan that we have fought with, why try to remain unknown?"

The day before his cousin had attempted to track the men who'd attacked Alexander. The trail of blood had led them to an abandoned encampment. By the items left behind, the group had left in a hurry. Probably to seek a healer to help with the two injured.

Since they'd no doubt bandaged up the men to staunch the blood loss, the trail soon became impossible to track as it merged onto a well-traveled road.

"PUT HIM ONTO the cart," Alexander instructed motioning to the body, then he looked to his men. "We will deliver him to Armandale, where I am sure he hailed from."

Alexander strode to his horse where an older man stood by. The man looked him up and down, by the dour expression found him lacking. "It is fortunate that there is a mysterious archer who does his best to save us from harm since the lot of ye have nae helped in the least."

"Aye, I am told a family was attacked near the river and a mysterious archer drove the attackers away," a woman called out.

He didn't give the woman any credence. Rumors of attacks were running rampant. Most of the time there were no bodies or witnesses coming forward to confirm it had occurred.

What could he say? That he was as frustrated as they were. It was proving impossible to find the men when they obviously had an entire village helping them to remain hidden. No matter how many times he and Munro had approached the people, no one in the village of Armandale was willing to divulge any information.

The dead man was loaded onto the back of a cart that was headed toward the village that used to be Mackinnon lands.

After defeating Laird Mackinnon and his warriors, the lands there had fallen under Clan Ross ownership. His brother, Munro, had taken over the keep and surrounding villages as a newly established laird.

Although he'd made a lot of progress gaining the loyalty of most of the people by treating them fairly and lowering taxes, there were still many who harbored ill will against Clan Ross. During the many years of battles, they'd lost fathers, sons, and brothers to Ross swords.

Alexander suspected the attackers were people who wanted to avenge the dead. No matter how noble these men thought their cause was, he would never allow the persecution of innocents. Like the man in the cart, those responsible for attacking his clan's people would all pay with their lives.

Leaving Knox behind to begin tracking the assailants, Alexander and several of his men rode in silence behind the wagon with the body. Each of them with the same set expression. Their jaws tight with frustration. Their gaze straight ahead.

"Is it possible that the same archer who saved this couple was the one who helped ye?" asked Hendry, one of his warriors.

"I doubt it," Alexander replied truthfully. "The arrows are different."

Hendry's eyebrows rose. "It could be we have our own band of men seeking vengeance on our side."

Alexander turned to his friend. "How does this person ken where the attackers will be? It seems impossible that this person just happens to be where the attacks occur?"

"Perhaps one of their group has turned against them," one of the guards replied.

"That idea has merit," Alexander told the guard.

Upon arriving at the village, the dead man was quickly identified, and they were told where his family lived.

The man had no wife and lived in a small cottage next to his parents' home. A group of people had already gathered, which meant they'd been informed of the man's death.

Two men approached the wagon and without a word began to unload the dead man. Alexander walked to them. "Ye dinnae seemed surprised to find out about this man's death." He studied the bearded man intently. "Who told ye?"

The man grunted, his eyes sliding to glance up at Alexander before looking back to the task at hand. "We were nae informed. The reason for the gathering is that we planned to go out and search for him."

"Aye, his parents were worried after he'd nae returned home."

The men's statement made sense; however, it was not believable. Especially since it was so late in the day and they'd yet to set out.

Walking behind the men carrying the body, Alexander stopped in the doorway of the humble home and peered into the dim interior.

An older woman, with a sorrowful expression, directed the men to place the body upon a table, whilst another man of about the same age as the woman motioned for Alexander to enter.

"Please sit down," the man stated in a raspy voice. "Thank ye for bringing my son home." Pulling out a dingy rag, the man mopped his face.

"Were ye aware he'd been killed whilst attacking innocent people?" Alexander asked.

There was a flash of annoyance on the man's face before he closed his eyes and took a deep breath. When he opened his eyes, they were calm. Flat. "We prayed he would be alive. We were just meeting to discuss a search." The man slid a look to the table his son had been placed upon.

"He was a good and loyal son," the man stated.

The phrasing of the man's words made Alexander hesitate. Why had the man chosen to describe his son as being loyal?

"Loyal to whom?" Alexander asked.

The old man shrugged, a smile curving his mouth his hand waving Alexander's question away as if it was of little importance. "Loyal to his family…"

It sounded as if the man was going to add something else, but he stopped and once again wiped his face.

Since the man persisted in his silence, Alexander tried a different question. "Who did he go riding with?"

"My son went alone," the man said and went to stand by the table where the body was. It was obvious he wouldn't say more.

Still, Alexander tried. "Ken that whoever is attacking the people of my clan will end up dead. I have a powerful army of trained warriors. These men…"—he motioned to the dead man—"have little chance against us."

The man met his gaze. "There is naught to be done about it, my son is dead, Laird Ross."

Alexander went to the doorway and spoke loudly so everyone could hear. "Ken this. Those who come against my people will be found and will pay with their lives."

Other than an exchange of glances, no one spoke. How could they be so blind and defiant? Their lives were so much better now that his brother had taken over. They had more freedom than ever. Their taxes were lower. Their lives were better. And yet, they persisted in their grudge against Clan Ross.

OUTSIDE THE HOME, he went to his horse and glanced around at the people who'd begun to gather.

He thought about repeating the threat but didn't. They were going to protect the men who were killing innocents, out of loyalty or fear. Perhaps both. It didn't matter, they'd not speak to him, especially not in front of witnesses.

His men, who'd patrolled the small area returned. By the looks of resignation, they too had been unsuccessful in gathering information.

"They insist the man had gone to hunt alone and that he's never ridden in a group," one of his warriors stated.

Hendry, a large muscular Ross warrior gave those gathered a menacing look. Several seemed to shrink under his direct gaze. "Tell those who enter our lands with ill intent that we are waiting for them."

Although the people seemed intimidated, no one said a word.

Riding back in the direction of where the attack had occurred, they met up with Knox, who'd tracked the blood droplets in the direction of Armandale, the village they'd just come from.

After Alexander informed Knox of everything that had occurred, the archer gave a weary sigh. "The easiest way to capture the attackers is to catch them in the act. Unfortunately, it is hard to predict where they go."

"We can set a trap," Alexander stated. He blew out a frustrated breath. "A warrior can dress as a farmer and drive a wagon on the roads near Armandale. We can have extra men on the back of the wagon, covered with hay or sacks."

"That could work," Knox said, his tone was without inflection. Meaning, his cousin doubted the plan would actually work.

"For now, I think they will take time before venturing out again. They have injuries and a death to deal with. I believe this mystery archer has served to deter any attacks for now," Alexander added. "That gives us time to plan for three wagons a day on different roads."

When they returned down the road to where the attack happened, it was as if nothing had occurred at all. The road was empty, and everyone had gone.

Knox frowned down at the dirt. "Several of us will remain here and plan the best routes to use and try to lure the attackers."

"I will leave ye to it then," Alexander replied.

When his personal guards attempted to come with him, he waved them away. "Help Knox, that is our priority at the moment. I am visiting a family and then going to the keep. There is nae any threat."

It was not long before he arrived on Maclaren lands. An expansive house sat centered between good-sized stables on one side and planted fields on the other. Sheep and several cows roamed freely on a green hillside through which a narrow stream flowed.

The house was built on a hill overlooking the shore. He'd always liked this particular place that was well served by the sea, a stream, and a pond that fed into it. In addition, there was plenty of land surrounding the house.

As he rode down the path toward the Maclaren home, memories of coming there during his childhood formed. He recalled running down that very path toward the house after a day of meandering in the woods with his brothers, Munro and Gavin, while the youngest, Cynden, and Nala did their best to keep up.

It had never occurred to him that Nala would one day leave for ten long years. As a matter of fact, when her parents had announced her imminent departure his youngest brother, Cynden, had been devastated at the loss of his close friend.

There was about a ten-year age difference between Alexander and Nala, so he'd not been too bothered by her leaving. On the cusp of manhood, he had other things on his mind. Proving himself, chasing after pretty young girls, and learning to properly wield a sword. Yet every so often, he'd thought about Nala and wondered what had become of her.

Upon arriving at the Maclaren home, a lad hurried to take the horse's reins, greeting him with open awe. "Laird, I will take good care of yer mount."

Alexander nodded at the lad. "Just water. He will be fed at the keep."

The front door opened as he approached, Nala's parents, Calum and Kamila, stood in the doorway.

Nala's mother was born on an island that Alexander had never heard of. Kamila described it as a place where all the people had brown skin and curly hair. She said the weather was always warm, the skies were clear, and the water a rich clear blue.

Her father, Calum, a tall man with bright blue eyes swept his arm toward the inside of the home. "I am delighted to see ye. Have nae seen much of ye since ye became laird," he said with a wide grin.

Kamila seemed genuinely glad he was there, greeting him with a warm hug. "I am so happy ye are here. I am planning a gathering to celebrate Nala's return. I planned to come visit yer mother, but time has gotten away from me. Be sure she knows to come along with ye and yer brothers."

He followed the couple into the main room, which was furnished quite uniquely compared to most of the other homes on Skye. According to his mother, they'd brought back many of the furnishings and decor from Kamila's home island.

"What brings ye," Nala's father asked. "Has something happened?"

Alexander glanced toward a doorway. "Have ye heard of the attacks?"

"Aye, a terrible thing," the man replied.

Kamila shook her head. "Such a pity. We hear it is on the other side of the lands, closer to Mackinnon lands."

"The last ones have been not too far from here," Alexander informed them.

At once the woman's eyes widened. "We should nae allow Nala to ride out alone."

"Where is she?" Alexander asked, glad they'd mentioned her.

Kamila shook her head. "Gone to Sencha MacTavish's house. They take turns visiting each other. She should return shortly. It is but a short distance to the MacTavish's. Do ye think it is safe?"

"Despite it being a short distance, she is alone, and it is dangerous. Perhaps from now on, send someone with her and advise Sencha's family to do the same," Alexander said knowing Nala would be cross at hearing that he warned her parents against her riding out alone.

A servant entered with a tray and placed mugs in front of Alexander and Calum. Kamila already had a small goblet in front of her, which he assumed was honeyed mead.

"Ye must stay for a meal," Calum stated.

Alexander took a drink of the fresh ale. "I cannae unfortunately. I was riding past and wished to inform ye of what occurred this morning. It was a husband and wife on their way home from Tokavaig. The attacks are unprovoked, for no apparent reason other than to create fear."

The couple exchanged worried looks. "What about yer men?" Kamila asked.

"Patrols are out every day. I assure ye, we are doing our best and they will be caught. Already several of them have been injured or killed." He left out the part where some of that was because of the mysterious archer.

Kamila clasped her hands in front of her chest. "We should send someone to escort her back home."

Alexander stood. "I am going in that direction," he lied. "I will see about Nala and bring her back."

There was a twinkle in her mother's eyes. "I am sure she will be glad to see ye after so long and also for the company of such a handsome young man like yerself."

Alexander frowned. Nala did not tell them they'd seen each other the day before. He realized she'd not because the lass kept her forays into the forest secret.

The couple followed him to the door, peppering him with questions about the attacks and about what his plans were. Finally, he was able to break away after reminding them he must see about Nala.

Alexander rode toward the MacTavish's home hoping not to have to knock on the door and have to visit the family, where once again he would be forced to drink ale and converse.

Relief flooded upon seeing Nala riding toward him. Atop the horse, back straight, hair pulled back, she seemed more a warrior than a delicate young lass.

Upon nearing, he noted the slight frown between her brows. She was definitely not happy to see him.

"Why are ye here?" It was not exactly a warm greeting, but he ignored it.

"Yer parents told me ye were out visiting the MacTavish's," he replied in an even tone, noting the long bow tied to the horse's saddle and the quiver of arrows slung across her back. There were plenty of arrows, so he wondered again if it might have been her who'd saved the couple.

She glanced down to her bow and lifted a challenging brow. "I was indeed at the MacTavish's most of the day."

"Nala, I must ask. Were ye on the east side of the forest this morning?"

"I left my home to visit my friend, Sencha, late morning," she replied motioning to the road that wound from where they were over a slight hill. "There is no forest along the way."

For a moment, he met her challenging gaze. "There was another attack. Or if I were to believe the rumors, there were two."

Her eyes widened. "That is horrible."

"Aye, it is," Alexander replied.

Her plump lips parted as she let out a breath. "Was anyone killed?" Her eyes met his in what seemed like genuine curiosity mingled with sadness.

The depth of her eyes pulled him in, and Alexander found it impossible to look away. "The couple attacked says they think an archer killed one of the attackers. The same archer saved them." He kept eye contact with her. "It made me think of how ye helped me."

She splayed her hand over her chest. "That is good news that the innocent people are safe. One of yer archers perhaps?"

Alexander had already questioned all his men. None had admitted to being the vigilante, but several admitted they would consider it now.

"Ye should nae be out riding alone. I informed yer parents about the attacks and yer father stated he will nae allow ye to be out without escort."

Nala frowned, eyes narrowing, but she remained silent. It was obvious she wasn't pleased that her future outings could possibly be limited. She guided her horse around him and continued in the direction of her home.

Her reaction was not surprising, as even as a child she'd been fiercely independent and obviously remained the same. Nala was a woman who had a hard time accepting being told what she could and couldn't do.

Alexander brought his horse alongside her ignoring the glare she directed at him. "I have every right to ensure the people on the lands are safe. It is my duty to the clan"

"I understand yer lairdship." Nala looked up at the sky. "Should ye not be out hunting for the attackers?"

He ignored the question. "If this vigilante is ye. It will only lead to dire consequences. I fear for ye. Allow my men and I to catch and do away with the attackers."

Nala opened her mouth to say something, but then she clamped it shut. The ire in her expression spoke volumes and he could sense she'd held her tongue only because he was her laird.

In a way he hated to dampen her spirit and although he did not have romantic feelings toward the lass, the need to protect her from harm was stronger than he could explain. Perhaps it had to do with knowing her since childhood.

She dismounted and pointed to the ground, so he followed suit, perplexed. She released the hold on her horse's reins and stomped closer to him. For a moment Alexander thought she planned to strike him. Instead, she pressed a finger into the center of his chest.

"I am nae a delicate lass that sits indoors simpering and sewing, or whatever it is they do. Not now, nor will I ever be happy to be kept away from this." She motioned around them, arms outstretched. "I am sure upon my return, Father will nae allow me to ride alone."

When she lifted up on her toes and once again pressed the same finger into his chest, Alexander's eyebrows shot up. He had to admit having her standing so close threw him off-balance. The intense way she glared up at him made him wonder what it would be like to kiss her. Had she been kissed before?

Just then he gathered she'd continued speaking and he'd not realized it.

"... Now because of these attacks, Mother will do her best to convince Father to send some sort of escort with me." She'd flattened her hand against his chest, not seeming to notice how intimate the gesture was. "I understand. Of course I do, but at the same time, I am very careful."

When she took a breath, Alexander bent at the waist to look her in the eye.

"What would it matter if ye had an escort. If ye are nae the vigilante, then it should nae be much of a hindrance."

Nala was silent for a moment. He almost smiled at how obvious it was that she considered how to reply.

When she didn't, he continued. "If ye continue to venture out alone, ye will be attacked. Perhaps ye can shoot from a tree, or hill, or even from a distance. But what will ye do if caught on horseback? Ye will be easy prey."

At a loss for words, Nala stared at him, eyes narrowing, breathing hard.

He covered her hand with his, and her eyes flew wide, and lips parted as she took a breath.

Surprisingly, Nala didn't move her hand but looked up at him with what looked like curiosity.

"Ye can be killed. Ye cannae possibly fight off a group of armed men. Do ye understand why I worry about ye?" Alexander asked in a soft voice.

Nala snatched her hand from under his and for a moment they stared at each other, neither wishing to be the first to look away.

Finally, Nala broke eye contact and went back to her horse. "I can ride the rest of the way without escort. Ye can see my house from here. I am sure ye have more important *lairdly* things to do than to follow me about." With a curt nod, she galloped away toward her home.

Alexander's lips curved; it would take a strong man to tame Nala. A docile Nala was not something he could picture, and he doubted any man would ever completely change her.

As she became smaller in the distance, Alexander frowned. Something about the lass made him want to protect her. At the same time of all the women he'd ever met, she was the one who needed protection the least.

"Go home," he said to his horse, whose ears flickered back at the sound of his command. It was doubtful his horse understood, but Alexander chose to think it did.

CHAPTER FOUR

"Is this really necessary?" Nala asked for what seemed like the hundredth time. Standing atop a stool as the seamstress poked and prodded her, adding last-minute stitches to a dress that was much too frivolous for the Highlands. In England, women wore gowns—like the deep blue creation she now donned—for every reason under the sun.

Nala thought it ridiculous that women often changed three times a day depending on what time it was. Nala had refused to change unless attending an event that required it. She wore the same dress she put on in the morning all day.

Her mother pursed her lips as she walked around Nala taking in every fold and the flow of the satiny skirt. "It is imperative that ye be the best dressed at the gathering. It is in yer honor after all."

Nala's lips curved. Not at what her mother said, but because of the rich island accent that always soothed her frayed nerves.

"Mother, I beg of ye. Dinnae speak of marriage to anyone. And dinnae state that ye wish me to be already married," Nala implored. "I dinnae wish every fool from far and wide coming forward to profess their feelings simply because of Father's wealth."

"Of course I wish ye to be already married. Most women

yer age already have two or three bairns." Kamila's eyes rounded in an attempt to look perplexed about Nala's request. "Ye should be grateful that I care."

The seamstress cut a thread and moved away. "Ye look beautiful, miss."

Nala frowned at the puffy tops of the sleeves. "I feel like an overly plump chicken."

"Ye look like a beautiful swan," her mother insisted with a satisfied purse of her lips. "I cannae wait for everyone's reactions."

"Dinnae be offended if the reaction is laughter," Nala said and tugged at the neckline in a futile attempt to cover the tops of her breasts. "If I bend my breasts will spill out."

"Stop protesting," her mother said walking toward the door. "I will have something sent up for ye to eat. Remain here."

When the door closed behind her mother and the seamstress, Nala went to the window and leaned out to look across the fields to the road. Already guests were arriving. She noted a group of men on horseback, several wagons, as well as a pair of coaches. Suddenly she was transported back to England, to the constant teas, galas, and other gatherings. They were not unhappy memories, in actuality, she'd enjoyed some of them. Still, her favorite moments were the quiet times with her cousins reading in the parlor.

However, their life consisted of so many social events that they rarely had a day of relaxation. It wasn't that she disliked the social events, what she could not stand for was the pageantry, the gossip, and the constant competing of women for men's attention. In high society, a man—especially a titled one—was the best prize a woman could ever have. Just the thought of it made her shake her head.

Now her mother planned something that was reminiscent of the social affairs she'd stayed away from. Those dedicated to finding a husband for the forlorn young women who'd not managed to find one on her own.

She let out a breath, wondering what her mother would be saying, the hints dropped to let mothers of eligible men know Nala was very much interested in marriage.

Nala scowled in thought. Who exactly of the men invited would garner her father's approval?

A carriage pulled by a team of beautiful sable horses appeared and she followed its progress. Next to the carriage rode two men, their huge warhorses unmistakable.

One was Knox Ross, the other Alexander. The laird stood out, with his impressive height, wide shoulders, and shoulder-length black hair. His cousin, Knox, was an attractive man. She'd not gotten to know him as well since he'd moved to Skye just before she'd left. The pair of times she'd seen him since returning, had been at Sencha's house. Knox and her brother had been close and often visited her father.

Although Knox had a slender build compared to Alexander, his shoulders and arms were muscular from archery. He had olive skin and light brown hair. His keen eyes were the palest green and were startling against his dark skin tone, giving him an exotic appearance.

MEMORIES OF THE many years she'd spent with the Ross lads before leaving flooded making her smile at seeing them approaching. Despite not seeing him in so long and the few recent interchanges, which had been Alexander mostly being protective, she remained fond of him.

A shiver went up her spine when she recalled how close they'd been when he'd attempted to admonish her for riding out alone. His emerald green eyes had darkened at one point, and she'd caught herself considering what it would be like to kiss him.

The thought had shaken her so badly, she'd had to get away from him as quickly as possible. What nonsense had caused that thought to form?

Surely it was the anger that had caused the romantic notions. There was no other explanation.

When Alexander and the carriage approached the house, he looked up as if sensing her watching him. Before he looked to her window, she moved away.

Something about him affected her so she decided it was best to keep from being alone with him. Thankfully there were several families attending the gathering, which meant it would be easy to avoid Alexander.

TO NALA'S SURPRISE, she was enjoying the gathering. She and Sencha sought out Ainslie Ross, Cynden's wife, and the trio huddled to talk about the other attendees. It was quite fun to find out who was involved with whom. Ainslie, who lived at Ross keep, was privy to what occurred within the gates and shared bits that had both Nala and Sencha hanging on her every word.

With a sheepish grin, Ainslie admitted to sitting near a

hearth in the great room, pretending to embroider, just to listen to the grievances brought to Alexander.

"It is better than storyteller's tale," Ainslie admitted sliding a look to where Cynden was. "I cannae believe the things some people come to him about."

Sencha, who adored rumors, sat forward in her chair, face flushed with excitement. "Does anyone come to speak to him about his men?"

Only Nala knew that Sencha's object of affection was Knox Ross. Admittedly the archer was very handsome; however, his roguish ways were legendary. Because of this, Sencha had decided she'd never act upon her feelings.

In Nala's opinion, Sencha deserved a man who took the time to get to know a woman and didn't spend his free time plundering whoever happened past.

Not that she knew for a fact that was how Knox passed his time, but whether he pursued women or was chased by them, the man needed to exercise more prudence.

"Who catches yer eye, Nala?" Ainslie asked with a twinkle in her eyes. "Hendry perhaps?" she asked eluding to a muscular warrior. "Or maybe a bigger prize… say… Alex?"

Nala's gaze flew across the room to where Alexander spoke with several men. As if sensing her perusal, his eyes met hers for a beat. She quickly looked back to her companions, who watched her with rapt attention. "I am nae interested in courtship. I need time to adjust to life on Skye."

"Interesting," Ainslie remarked. "Ye have certainly caught the laird's attention."

That her cheeks became hot was annoying. Nala waved the words away. "If he looks to me, it is because he is cross with me."

"What happened?" Sencha asked, her eyes moving between her and Alexander.

"Nothing of note," Nala replied. "He suggested that I be escorted when visiting ye, I informed the laird that I didnae require such nonsense as the road between our homes is safe enough. I am nae sure he agreed."

Sencha gasped and Ainslie continued to watch her with a knowing smile. The woman was not much older than her, perhaps even the same as her two and twenty. Yet Ainslie seemed to believe she was more knowledgeable in heart matters.

"We should go out to the garden," Nala suggested. "It is nae too cold."

When they stood, Nala slid a glance toward where Alexander was. To her consternation, her father was speaking with him. Before she could look away, she noted her father gesture toward his study then he and Alexander headed in that direction.

What did Alexander have to speak to her father about in private? Hopefully it wasn't about her unescorted outings. Or worse, that Alexander suspected she was the avenging archer.

ALEXANDER FOUND IT hard to keep from stealing glances at Nala. Gone was the wildling on horseback who wore her hair in a braid down her back and clothing that resembled more what a man would wear.

The woman who seemed to glide across the room was a siren. Her dark tresses were swept up, displaying her graceful neck. Jewels hung from her ears and although she kept the challenging look in her expression, her beautiful features were accentuated by the low neckline.

When she walked, the folds of her gown swayed side-to-side, calling attention to the curves of her body. He'd done his best to keep from openly gawking, but in that dress it proved impossible. The swells of her breasts were perfectly displayed, from the delicate mounds, the eye was drawn to her cinched waist.

Whoever had chosen the gown had done extremely well, if the intent was to catch men's attention.

At the moment, Nala walked away toward the doors leading to the side garden and he almost rushed over to insist she donned a shawl, or preferably a cape. A thick long furry one that covered everything would be best.

When Knox elbowed him, Alexander realized he'd been watching Nala much too long, and he immediately scanned the room until finding another woman. Unfortunately, the woman was about eighty years old and currently coughing so violently that he wondered if she'd drop dead.

Nala's mother and his own rushed to the old woman attempting to help her catch her breath. Finally the woman seemed to settle, and conversations resumed.

"Alexander, a word." Calum Maclaren stood before him, the older man looking up at him. Although Calum was not a short man, he had to look up to Alexander as he was taller than most men.

"Of course," Alexander said nodding to Knox, who greeted the older man.

He followed Nala's father to a study and sat when the man

motioned to a chair. Calum poured two glasses of whiskey, handing one to Alexander.

After settling in another chair, Calum drank and waited for Alexander to do the same.

"Is something amiss?" Alexander asked. From the man's relaxed expression, it was difficult to surmise what the man wished to speak about.

"I hear good things about ye. I am sure yer father would be proud of how ye are handling the lairdship." Calum smiled softly. "He never worried, ye see. Always said he was sure about yer abilities to take over the clan."

Alexander knew his father and Calum had been close friends. Every time he met with Calum it was inevitable for him to think of his father. There were many times he'd catch the two men with a dram of whiskey in deep conversations that sometimes lasted hours. Many a time, they would just sit in companionable silence, enjoying each other's company.

"I do miss him," Alexander said and took another sip of whiskey.

Calum looked at the amber liquid in his own glass for a bit. "There are times when I wish to share things with him and have to remind myself he is gone."

Alexander spoke wishing to change the subject. "I am grateful to ye for yer words of encouragement. As of late, I have felt as if I am failing my people. The attacks have continued without us able to find out who the culprits are."

"A difficult task to have so much responsibility on yer shoulders. Which brings me to one of the reasons I wished to speak with ye."

His attention grabbed; Alexander met the man's gaze. "I

am listening."

Calum took his time speaking. First he swirled the amber liquid in the glass studying it, then lifted his gaze to Alexander. "When yer father was alive, he often said that lairdship is not the work of just one man. A good laird surrounds himself with wise council. Ye have been trying to do it alone. Ye must see that although ye are a very judicious young man, ye lack experience in some matters."

The truth of the words almost made Alexander flinch. Truthfully, he'd forgotten about the council. There had been so much happening. Between his brothers' marrying, warring first with the Mackinnons, then the MacLeods, and now the attackers, he'd only been able to concentrate on one day at a time.

"I had not considered it," he admitted, lowering his head. "In truth I am exhausted." Alexander kept his gaze down, not wishing for Calum to see that tears threatened. It had been so long since he'd been given advice from someone like the man before him. Someone who was a fatherly figure. It made him yearn for his father's wisdom.

He blinked, hoping the moistness would dissipate. "Will ye help me?"

Calum chuckled. "I didnae consider I was giving myself the position as part of the council. But if ye wish it then aye, I can do so."

"Who else do ye suggest?" Alexander lifted the glass to his lips and drained it. Calum refilled it and poured more for himself.

The man looked into the fire. "I suggest Liam Murray, and perhaps the constable Donald Brown. He is a good man."

THEY CONTINUED SPEAKING for a bit longer about who would be good members of a six-man council. As they discussed, Alexander could feel the weight on his shoulders lesson. Perhaps it was the third glass of whiskey or the fact he would have help in leading the people, but he began to relax.

"We should rejoin the festivities," Calum said. "Kamila will be looking for us."

Before Alexander could stand, Calum held out a hand. "I hesitate to bring this up, but there has been something that I do wish to discuss. Perhaps not tonight, but I would like to come to the keep and speak to ye about it."

The tone of the man's voice piqued Alexander's curiosity. "Of course, ye are welcome at any time." He couldn't keep from asking. "What do ye wish to speak to me about?"

The man stood and Alexander followed suit.

When Calum's lips curved, he felt his own shoulders lower with relief that whatever the man wished to talk to him about was not dire. So used to bad news, it was what he'd come to expect.

Calum looked down the corridor as if to ensure no one would overhear. He spoke in a low tone. "I wish to confer with ye about my daughter. She requires a husband."

"Err... Aye... of course." Alexander wasn't sure what the man meant. Did he expect Alexander to marry Nala? Or to help find the lass a husband? Neither option sat well with him at the moment. He was not meant to be a matchmaker for the clan's people. It was a task his mother was better suited for.

Not waiting for a reply, the older man walked to where his guests mingled and was called to join a conversation with two men. Alexander took the pair in, one was a farmer, the other a merchant, neither was married. He scanned the room, noting which other unmarried men were there.

Was this a gathering so that Nala could choose a husband? He searched the room and noted that Nala had returned from outside. She stood beside her mother, a frown marring her face. She craned her neck and looked about, the crease between her brows in place. When their gazes met, her gaze swept over him, as if assessing his attire. Then she looked away, a slight lift to the corners of her lips.

Alexander walked to where Nala stood. "May I have a word?"

Her mother smiled broadly. "Go, lass. See what his lairdship wishes."

Nala bit her bottom lip, then gave a curt nod. "Of course." Her voice was sugary sweet, making Alexander wonder what she was up to.

They walked away from the group. He wasn't sure exactly how to approach the subject of Nala getting married, so he decided directness was the best approach.

"Ye are of age to marry. Have ye given thought to whom ye wish to…" Before he could continue, Nala interrupted, speaking in a low hiss.

"Why would I speak to ye about this? Did my father say something to ye?" Her eyes bore into him. A flush pinkened her cheeks, something he'd noticed during their previous interactions.

He decided on a different approach. "I ask because yer father may have mentioned something about it."

Rising to her toes to better meet his gaze, she glared. "I am nae interested in marriage to anyone. If Father brings it up again, assure him no man would wish to be married to someone like me."

"Like ye?"

"Spirited," she quipped. At the pronouncement, she seemed to realize how close their faces were. Her widened eyes lowered, hesitating on his lips before she turned her head. "Is there anything else ye wish to speak to me about *Laird*?" Nala practically spit out the last word.

"Nothing, for now." Alexander took her elbow. "I will escort ye back."

It was not the first time he'd touched her, yet, this time, something about the gesture seemed intimate, almost proprietary.

Admittedly the lass had grown to be a beauty beyond compare. However, as he had no desire to marry anytime soon, he refused to consider any thoughts beyond the fact that he enjoyed her independent disposition and the way she spoke her mind. And the fact she had an alluring body did not go unnoticed.

Alexander cleared his throat as they approached her mother.

It was slight, but he felt Nala attempt to pull her elbow free. He didn't release it, interested to see what she did next.

With a pleasant expression, she smiled at their mothers and the other women they stood with. "It is almost sunset, we should go see it."

As one the women turned to look toward the doorway, it was then Nala stomped on his foot, her heel thrusting with force onto the top of his boot.

Alexander let out a loud groan causing the women to turn

back and give him questioning looks.

"What happened?" Kamila asked, reaching out to him. "Are ye unwell?"

All he could do was clamp his teeth together to keep from spewing an obscenity. "Dinnae be alarmed. I recalled something important that I forgot to do. It is all."

"Ye should take care of the important thing immediately," Nala said with a wide-eyed innocent expression.

With a nod at the women, he walked away doing his best not to favor the aching foot.

Whomever the minx married, the hapless man would live to regret it.

CHAPTER FIVE

While dressing in attire suitable for riding, Nala went over the activities of the night before. Despite her lack of enthusiasm at her mother inviting so many marriageable men, she'd enjoyed the evening. Her only regret was having stomped on Alex's foot. He would get back at her, she was sure of it. For the next few days, she'd have to be on guard and ensure to keep her wits about her.

Surprisingly, he'd not told her parents about her exploits in the forest. Of course, it was not a good tale for a man to share. How she'd saved him from attackers. The laird of Clan Ross, rescued by a lass. The corners of her lips tugged upward. It was comical, she supposed.

Once she finished lacing her leather boots, Nala tossed her quiver over her left shoulder, grabbed the bow, and slipped from the room. Skirting past her mother's sitting room and down the stairs she hesitated once reaching the bottom of three floors. Flat against the wall, she peered from her hiding place. A quick glance assured her there was no one about, so she raced outside and made her way around the house, the entire time staying close to the exterior walls to keep from being seen through the windows.

She left the shelter of the house and ran to the stables finding the stableman, Finis, sitting on a stool, back to the wall, and feet up on a stack of logs. He snored softly as he often napped after the midday meal.

Nala skirted him and grabbed a saddle. Then quickly as possible made her way out to the corral to find Shadow.

It wasn't until she rode over the hill just north of her home that Nala was able to let out a long breath of relief to have gotten away unnoticed.

Her parents were fair and reasonable people. She understood why her father insisted she take the stableman with her when out riding, but the man was older and rarely rode the horses. She'd be hindered having to wait on him and more importantly, he would inform her father if she went anywhere other than directly to Sencha's house.

For goodness sake, she was two and twenty. It seemed like bairns barely out of diapers had more freedom than women. Where was the fairness in that?

It was a windy day, and she was glad to have worn a cape. Although the article of clothing would make it hard to climb a tree and hide. She looked in the direction of the forest and then to her friend's house. Sencha would be expecting her, they had much to discuss about the night before.

She'd excused herself to go to her room to write letters to her friends in London, so it would be at least two hours before her parents discovered her gone. She decided to go for a short ride, then to Sencha's. By the time either the stableman or her father rode out to find her, she'd be at her friend's home.

Nala considered Alexander's warnings. If she were caught alone astride, she'd be an easy target for the group of evil bastards that were going about killing people who could not defend themselves.

At the same time, old Finis, wouldn't be much help. If anything, the poor man would serve as a distraction. Someone to leave behind as she escaped. Not that she'd do that, but it was highly doubtful the man could outrun anything.

Nala let out a huff and turned Shadow in the direction of Sencha's house. Alexander was right, it was not safe, too many attacks had occurred.

"What have ye been doing today?" Sencha greeted Nala with a wide smile. "I expected ye would have an escort."

It was impossible to lie to Sencha, at the same time, Nala had not told her the entire truth of what she'd done. It was best that her friend did not know every detail that occurred.

"I should have waited, but the thought of it annoyed me. I know it may nae be safe, but I am careful. I am sure once Mother finds out I rode here alone and will soon send Finis to fetch me."

"Ye are rebellious to a fault," Sencha stated, crossing her arms. "Anything can happen to ye, and no one would be the wiser."

"What has our Nala done now?" Sencha's mother walked into the room.

Sencha and Nala exchanged looks. Her friend spoke. "She insists on never wishing to marry. Her mother is most cross."

"Oh, Nala," the older woman soothed. "It is nae that ye dinnae wish to marry. It is that ye have yet to meet the man who will change yer mind."

"That may be true," Sencha said. "The right man will instantly change the way ye think."

"Bah," Nala replied. "There is nae such a man."

The older woman laughed and looked at her with a knowing expression. "It will happen, ye will see."

They began discussing the gathering at Nala's house the night before. Mostly they talked of which men and women seemed interested in one another and of course what Knox and Alexander did while there. Nala was swept up in the conversation, welcoming the distraction from thinking about her future.

By the time Finis arrived, she was prepared to return home.

Her mother kept stealing worried glances at Nala the following day as they headed to Keep Ross for a visit. "I would have preferred if ye would have worn something more colorful than dull serviceable clothing."

Nala peered out the window of the coach. "I prefer to be comfortable. Besides those large stone buildings are always drafty and cold."

Despite worries about her mother once again attempting matchmaking, Nala looked forward to seeing the keep again.

"I am sure some changes have been made since I was last there," Nala added.

"Aye, it is bigger. The rooms are kept warm with large hearths, tapestries, and rugs on the floors."

Nala peered out the window at the passing shoreline, noting fishing boats bobbing in the water. It was a sunny day, as spring gave way to summer. Soon the days would stretch longer, and the weather would be warmer.

A narrow bridge led to the entrance gates that were guarded by warriors. Atop the surrounding keep walls archers kept watch. Though for some reason they did not seem menacing to Nala.

With the sea behind it and a steep cliff to the right side of the keep, it was a secure place for refuge from attacks. Somehow Alexander's home matched him, a mixture of savage and beauty, security and danger.

They rode into the courtyard where they were greeted by stable lads, who assisted both Nala and her mother from the coach.

At the front door, Lady Ross and Ainslie greeted them warmly. Ainslie's eyes twinkled with mischief. "I cannae wait to talk."

Nala couldn't help but grin at her, knowing her friend would share tidbits of whatever she'd overheard in the great room.

"I am so glad ye came," Alexander's mother stated, her eyes bright. "I'd just complained to Ainslie that I didnae wish to spend the afternoon doing chores."

Nala had always loved Lady Ross, even as a child. She found her to have a calming presence.

They walked into the great room and Nala's breath caught. She'd forgotten the elegance of Scottish castles. The majesty of the clan coat of arms on the walls, and the beauty of intricately carved tables, benches, and chairs used for dining. The arched windows on two walls allowed plenty of sunlight into the space, giving the room an airy feeling, not cloistered and dark like most castles with their stone walls.

On the opposite side from where they stood, Alexander sat at the high board with men on either side. Her father, who'd arrived a day earlier, was also there. She drew her gaze away—before he caught her looking—and took in a hearth so huge, a man could easily stand inside of it.

Fire in the hearth kept the room at a pleasant temperature so there was no need to wear cloaks or even shawls.

Nala and her mother followed the Ross women to sit in overstuffed chairs in front of the hearth. Lady Ross motioned a servant over and asked that bread, cheese, and honeyed mead be brought for them.

Without looking Nala sensed Alexander's gaze and she turned to look toward the high board. Alexander gave a barely perceptible nod when their eyes met, then he returned his attention to the pair of men who stood before the council.

Ainslie, ever perceptive, caught Nala looking. "Those two are nothing of note. They wish to have land to sow."

Noting there were several people standing about waiting, she couldn't help but to acknowledge how heavy the burden of being laird was. Yet, it seemed, Alexander kept his attention on those in front of him, not seeming to hurry them along.

"Ye can have a small sector. See the scribe about it. More will be given if ye produce a good harvest. It is late in the season now, so I give ye until the end of next harvest," he told the men.

Nala lost track of what the women spoke about, her interest on the proceedings, as each person or group approached Alexander. She understood why Ainslie enjoyed sitting and listening to this.

More than anything, she admired the way Alexander proceeded over each task. He listened intently, asked questions, and referred to the other men sitting next to him before considering how to proceed.

Ainslie and the other women stopped speaking when a

woman cried out. Hands over her face, she cried as her husband accused her of adultery.

"I was never unfaithful," she said between shaky breaths and hiccups. "He wishes to do away with me so that he can take up with a harlot from the village. We have three bairns and very little to call our own. What will I do?"

"Ye should go back to yer parents. Or to whomever ye are lying with," the man said, pointing a finger at her. When she attempted to reach for her husband, he shoved her away. The children surrounding them began to cry, a very young one clinging to his mother's skirts.

"Oh, goodness," Lady Ross said in a sad voice. "That poor woman."

The room went silent when Alexander stood, rounded the table, and walked closer to the family. Every eye followed each of his movements as he lowered to one knee and spoke to the oldest child, a boy, who looked to be about ten.

"Are ye home with yer mother every day?"

The boy nodded, eyes wide. "Aye, Laird."

"Have ye ever seen a man come to yer home when yer father is nae there?"

The boy shook his head sliding a look to his father. "Nae. Never Laird."

"Does yer mother ever leave ye and yer siblings to steal away?"

Once again, the boy stole a glance at his father who glared down at him.

"Dinnae look at him," Alexander said in a low voice. "Look at me."

"Wherever Ma goes she always takes us with her, Laird. To

the market, to visit the old lady, Una, even when we dinnae wish to go."

Alexander rose and towered over the husband, whose eyes rounded. "When exactly is it yer wife has time to be unfaithful in yer estimation?"

The man huffed, taking a step back. "I cannae see her all day. I work. Perhaps she is nae, but she is failing as a proper wife."

Alexander shook his head, his disappointment obvious. "Marriage is a privilege, nae a burden. Yer bairns are a gift, nae a hindrance. If ye persist in wishing to send yer family away, then ye cannae remain in the house. Ye will go live elsewhere and no longer have rights to work the lands."

The man's mouth fell open. "Ye dinnae understand, Laird. I have done nothing wrong."

Alexander motioned to the two men who'd asked for land to plant. "I can grant the lands to them."

The man looked around the room, seeming at a loss for words. "That would nae be fair."

"Is it fair for yer wife and bairns to be sent away because ye are lying with another woman? That ye send them away and leave them without safety, food, or home?"

Managing to finally look abashed, the man looked at his feet. "Nae, Laird."

"Go home and work yer land and care for yer family. I will send my men around to ensure yer wife and bairns remain well cared for. If not, then ye will be banished." Alexander waited for the man to meet his eyes. "Am I understood?"

The man nodded. "Aye, Laird." He motioned for his wife, who lifted the smallest one to her arms and grabbed another's hand to follow after him.

The eldest child lingered and gave Alexander a solemn look. "One day I will be a guard for ye," the boy said. "I will care for my mum until then."

"I am sure ye will," Alexander replied placing a hand on the boy's skinny shoulder. He spoke to the boy in a whisper so that only the child would hear. Standing straighter the boy turned and followed after his family.

Nala couldn't drag her gaze away from Alexander. The same man who was stern with his clan's people giving orders and mandates, took time to speak to a child, openly praising him. It was rare that men took time to consider young ones, that Alexander took time from his duties to do so... well it was inspiring.

When he returned to sit at the sideboard he motioned to a man. "What is it this time Lionel?"

"Ye see why I enjoy sitting here and listening?" Ainslie said, breaking Nala's attention away from what occurred before the laird.

"Aye," Nala acquiesced. "It is certainly interesting."

Lady Ross stood and smoothed her skirts. "Let us go out to the garden. It is too beautiful a day to remain indoors."

As they walked through the great room to the main doorway, murmurs arose. Nala was fully aware that she and her mother didn't look like anyone else on the isle. Her mother's skin was a deep brown, Nala's a lighter shade, but still darker than most of the paler skinned people of Skye.

The fact that her mother didn't seem phased by looks of open curiosity and sometimes dislike, never ceased to amaze Nala.

When she was young she hated being different from everyone else. Her hair was curlier, her skin darker, lips fuller. She stood out whenever going places about the isle, whether markets, gatherings, or fetes.

The seasons in England helped as she met several other women with features like hers. Despite being different—or as her aunt insisted "exotic"—because of her father's wealth, she was popular with suitors. That was until she disregarded their attempts, turning down all offers.

She wasn't so naïve as to not understand that men found her attractive, and yet, at times, she wondered if it was her beauty or that she was what would be considered unusual. Looking at some of the onlookers' faces, she relaxed when she saw nothing more than curiosity and warmth.

The garden was surprisingly large and well maintained, especially when Lady Ross confided that she and a young servant girl were the only ones who worked in it.

"I dinnae care for someone traipsing about who does nae ken about flowers," she quipped as they strolled past fragrant flowers.

Nala stopped to admire the collection of contrasting colors. Some were growing from bushes, others spilling from planters hung on wooden arches built to provide shade.

"I could spend hours here," Nala said looking about. "It is absolutely beautiful."

When her mother and Lady Ross exchanged a conspiratorial look, the hairs on the back of her neck stood alert.

"It is interesting that ye would say that," Lady Ross said with a wide smile. "Please stay for a long visit. Ainslie could use yer company as I am about to go and visit family for a fortnight or two."

Nala's mouth fell open, but no sound came out.

Of course, that had to be the reason her father had come a pair of days early. It wasn't just to be part of the newly formed council, he no doubt spoke to Alexander about her staying there.

She couldn't possibly remain there; around Alexander, who affected her in a way she wasn't prepared to think about. And then there was the fact that this was probably part of her mother's plot to find her a husband.

"What a fabulous idea, of course Nala accepts yer gracious invitation," her mother interjected when Nala had yet to reply.

Words were stuck in her throat. There was no greater offense in the Highlands than to turn down an invitation by a member of the laird's family to visit.

Despite the trepidation, Nala managed to force the corners of her lips to inch up. "Thank ye for the kind invitation, of course I would love to remain for a bit."

"Ye have known my sons since bairns. I remember ye and Cynden spending hours playing in the courtyard." Lady Ross' face warmed at the memory. "Those were delightful times."

Nala was sure the woman thought of her husband, and she hated to see the hint of sadness in her eyes.

"Cynden led me to trouble many times," she said, and Lady Ross chuckled.

"He did indeed."

They continued strolling through the garden and then sat under an umbrella of shade provided by a huge tree that hung over the short wall. As the discussion turned to what had occurred with the attack of Clan MacLeod and the assailants from Armandale, Nala was astonished at how well-informed both Lady Ross and Ainslie were.

Lady Ross had delicate sensibilities, often taking to her bedchamber for long periods when battles or other strife occurred. So when she spoke of the challenges the clan faced in a calm tone, it surprised Nala. Perhaps over the years, the woman had changed.

"I imagine it has been very difficult for ye, surrounded by battles as well as the attacks on the clan," Nala said to the woman. "Most of us are nae aware of what occurs, other than through messengers or gossip."

Lady Ross looked toward an open field where guards practiced with swords. "I detest violence. But it seems the way of men."

In the field, men grunted as they thrust weapons at one another. They were well trained, formidable, and effortlessly intimidating. It was a good thing they were so threatening since their primary purpose was to defend an entire clan.

"Aye, some men seem to seek violence. And then it is up to other men to protect us from it," her mother added.

Nala let out a breath and considered that not all protectors were men.

CHAPTER SIX

It was late in the afternoon before Alexander finally finished work for the day. There had been so many seeking his attention that day, more than usual. People in fear were emotional and acting before thinking. Many of the issues brought to him could have been easily solved if the parties involved would have negotiated without screaming or punching.

He stretched and studied the great room. There were only a few people about, those who waited for someone to fetch them or had been ordered to remain by him.

"Why do ye nae look tired," Cynden said, his face drawn. "I cannae take another day like this one."

Alexander chuckled. "Yer wife keeping ye up? Perhaps ye should sleep in another room tonight."

His brother searched the room for Ainslie. "She is with child," he murmured in a low tone. "She told me last night and then began crying for no reason."

"That is strange," Alexander replied. "Is she nae glad?"

Cynden scratched his head. "Said she was crying with happiness."

The brothers frowned unable to understand the ways of women.

Calum Maclaren approached. "My wife and I will be on

our way, as soon as I find her." The man's eyes were bright. "I will be here every three days as we discussed."

It was obvious that the man was glad to regain his role on the council.

"I am glad for yer guidance. It is a great help. Thank ye for bringing the need for a council to my attention," Alexander said as the man waved away his words and walked from the room.

His brother followed soon after, rushing up the stairs, probably to sleep. Alexander almost reminded him that he was supposed to go on patrol early the next morning but decided against it. Cynden would not shirk his duties.

WALKING TO THE kitchen to find something to eat, he considered what Calum had spoken to him about. The man had arrived the day before and they'd met in Alexander's study.

Nala would be staying at the keep for a season in hopes that she'd find a husband. Her father expected that he help facilitate a betrothal.

The lass could easily fetch suitors. Just earlier as she crossed the room, every eye followed her progress. And yes, it was partly because of her exotic looks, but mainly the men's gaze moved over her body, then locked on her face. She was a beauty to behold.

"Laird!" Cook exclaimed when he entered the kitchens. "Come sit. Ye have nae eaten a bite since rising. Ye must be famished." The woman fussed over him, directing him to sit in the servants' dining room. A large sturdy table with eight chairs and a well-built sideboard were the only furnishings in the room.

His entire life, he'd often come there, liking to watch the hustle and bustle of activity in the adjoining kitchen as he ate. It was no different this time. A bowl of steaming meat and potatoes was placed before him, along with crusty bread and a crock of creamy butter. A large mug of ale finished the presentation.

Left to his own, he ate whilst the clanging of dishes filled the air around him. It was then he allowed his shoulders to fall, and he took a moment to close his eyes. There was much to do yet that day.

For the time being, he would not go on patrol as he was needed there at the keep. Duties that would take days to complete, if not weeks. The departure of warriors loaned to him by his cousin on Uist and the arrival of the new warriors from Uist to take their place. Along with the horses that would have to be exchanged as well.

Not to mention the plan they had in place to trap the attackers would begin the next day. He prayed it worked.

A voice caught Alexander's attention. It was Nala. She spoke to Cook, and he listened to see why the lass was in the kitchens.

"...get some carrots? I wish to give some to the horses." Nala's voice was rich with husky tones that made it unmistakable. "Thank ye."

Had the minx brought her horse? Alexander was sure she would have arrived with her mother in a coach. He'd noticed her earlier in the great room. Although she was not dressed in finery, neither was she dressed to ride. She was definitely up to something.

He took the last chunk of bread and used it to sop up the

remnants of food in his bowl and ate it. After drinking the last of the ale, he leaned back in the chair.

Seeming to have the keenest of senses, Cook appeared. "Would ye like more, Laird?"

Alexander looked at the older woman and shook his head. "Ye dinnae have to call me laird. Ye raised me from a bairn."

"Aye, but I must set the example for the younger servants. Else, they get ideas," the stubborn woman insisted. Then she bent and pressed a kiss to his brow. "But ye will always be my sweet lad."

He left the kitchen and walked out the side door to the courtyard and caught sight of Nala making her way to the corrals.

For a moment he considered whether to follow her or see about his duties. However, curiosity won out, and he crossed the courtyard toward where she was.

She leaned on the fence and looked over the horses. When a brown gelding neared, Nala fished a carrot from her skirt's pocket and held it out for the animal to nibble. "Ye are a beauty, but too small," she said to the horse, who nudged her hand hoping for another treat.

"Are ye planning yer escape already?" Alexander asked, pressing his lips together to contain a smirk when she visibly jumped.

Keeping her attention on the horses, she didn't turn to him. "I like horses. Ye have a varied assortment."

There were about five and ten horses in the corral, some grazing, others standing under a shade tree, probably sleeping. "We breed some for riding, some for battle, and still others simply because they are a beautiful breed."

"Do ye sell them?" She finally turned to look at him.

For a moment he was lost in the depths of her thickly lashed eyes. Tearing his own away to look to the horses, he nodded. "Aye, we sell those like the one ye just fed."

"My father spoke to ye." Her statement was flat. "Ye ken how I feel about marriage."

"There were more foals than usual this year. Six in all. Four of them will be trained for battle."

Nala gave him a puzzled look and then turned to look at the horses.

Alexander continued, "It is the way of things. That each horse has a place and a purpose. They have little choice in most things, except temperament. I personally get to know each of the horses to help with figuring out what they are best suited for."

He looked at Nala. "I am nae so arrogant to ken that I am always right. But in all things, I do my best."

Understanding dawned and Nala's brow pinched and her jaw set. "I am nae a horse, Laird."

"It is very obvious ye are nae a horse, but a beautiful woman with a strong temperament. I am nae sure what type of man would be brave enough to marry ye."

A harsh laugh sounded as Nala looked skyward and then to him. "There is yer answer. 'Tis best to leave me be."

"I will nae do that," Alexander replied. "Do ye not consider what it will truly be like to have someone in yer life that will always be there for ye? Everyone has those moments when we need someone."

He'd not meant to say the second part, and his words surprised even him.

When Nala's lips curved, he understood Nala caught the slip. "Is that so? Are there times when ye are lonely, Laird? So lonely ye wish for someone to hold yer hand?" She mocked, with a playful batting of lashes. "Do ye pine for a lass to soothe yer delicate soul?"

It was his turn to huff at the comment. "That is nae what I meant."

"What did ye mean?" She lifted to her toes. "Poor Alexander, needs to be comforted."

"Would ye do it? Would ye comfort me?" he teased back expecting she'd be shocked.

Instead she grinned, lifted her hand, and slid it down the side of his face. "There, there."

The touch sent tingles of awareness through him, but he refused to show any emotion. At his lack of reaction, Nala pressed further, cupping his jaw. "Would ye like Nala to kiss it and make it better?"

Alexander narrowed his eyes despite wanting to ask that she never lower her hand. "Enough."

"Hmm, I think ye dinnae mean it," Nala said, then to his astonishment she pressed her lips to his jaw. "Now, go on a be a good laird."

Frozen to the spot as Nala turned on her heel and briskly walked back to the house, Alexander finally let out a breath. To his consternation, he'd become aroused, his cock hardening and pressing against the front of his breeches.

What was he a lad of ten and five?

Letting out a grunt, he blew out breaths, willing the damn thing to soften. At noting the sway of Nala's hips, his cock twitched, and he cursed out loud.

"What is it, Laird?" One of the stable lads hurried toward him. "Do ye require a horse?"

"Nae," he replied in a husky tone. "Perhaps a swim in a cold loch is more what I need."

KNOX AND FOUR men came to the corrals. His cousin looked at him and then turned to look in the direction of the house. "What are ye doing?"

"Considering who would marry Nala Maclaren."

"Nae me. Dinnae ask. I will marry when my beard turns gray." Knox shrugged. "There will be many who would. She is bonny. Nae, not bonny. Nala is a rare beauty, she is."

"There is the matter of her temperament," Alexander stated. "She is fiery and refuses to stay at home. Instead goes out riding despite warnings about the attackers."

Behind them, the warriors began saddling horses, preparing for the last patrol of the day. Knox stole a look toward the house. "I know of one man who could possibly take on the beauty."

Alexander's eyebrows rose in surprise. He'd yet to think of anyone. "Who?"

"Ye. Of course. I doubt ye can tame the wildling, but the mantle of being a laird's wife would."

Chuckling at his expression, somewhere between horror and shock, Knox walked away whistling a happy tune.

Alexander frowned at his cousin's back. Surely there was someone who was worthy of Nala. There had to be. He considered his guardsmen. But came up short. He'd considered Knox, but his cousin was not keen on being ordered. He had no doubt Knox would leave on a bìrlinn without a destination, rather than marrying a woman not of his choosing.

"Wait," Alexander caught up with Knox. "Are ye setting up a trap today?"

"Aye," Knox said nodding. "The wagon is just now leaving. We have a woman who volunteered to come along and ride with Hamus. We will spread out and hide where we can. They will nae attack near trees, I am sure of it. The mysterious archer lurks among them."

"It could be the injuries will keep them from riding. But it has been a few days," Alexander said.

Shortly thereafter, four men on horseback left. The fifth man guided the wagon out of the gates and next to him was one of the women servants. *A brave lass.*

"Laird," his scribe hurried over. "We are ready to discuss the tallies of accounts." The younger man was slim, his clothing always clean, and his hair neatly brushed back from his face and held in place with a strip of fabric. His scribe was fastidious with accounts and rarely forgot anything, which suited Alexander well.

The entire time his scribe and the storeroom man went over ledgers, Alexander's mind kept returning to what Knox had said. That he should marry Nala.

Just a few weeks earlier, he'd insisted he was not the least bit interest in marriage and yet when Knox suggested it, Alexander was shocked. Not at the suggestion, but at the fact that he found the idea appealing.

Several times, he had to ask the men to repeat what had been said, until he admitted to not being able to concentrate.

He stalked from the house, down the steps to the shoreline

and walked to where the waves lapped gently on the rocks. Dragging his tunic over his head, he then removed his breeches and dove into the frigid water.

The shock of the cold made him gasp, but the feel of the water against his skin was tantalizing and just what he needed. Alexander swam to a good depth and then continued sideways for a while, and then back. His arm muscles strained to move him forward, his legs pushing him to continue.

Turning toward the shore, he was finally able to touch the bottom, and he walked forward until the water was waist-high. He pushed his hair back from his face, deciding it was time to cut it as he usually did every summer. Once he rinsed the salt water from his body, he would seek out the stablemaster and ask that he cut his hair.

Just then movement caught his attention. A lass walked along the shoreline toward the village. Alexander recognized her and rushed to dress. Nala was up to something, and he was going to find out what.

His clothes clung to his wet body, and he tugged at the tunic, then gave up and followed the stubborn woman. She was outside the keep walls *alone* after all the warnings he'd given her. As his guest, she was under his protection and no matter how independent, the lass had to learn to comply with the rules of living in the keep.

She didn't seem to have a destination in mind because she stopped, shaded her eyes with her right hand, and stared off into the distance. A few moments later, she bent and picked up something that she threw into the water.

"Nala." He'd caught up to her and took her by the arm. "What are ye doing? Ye cannae go about alone. I have told ye more than once."

Wide-eyed, she looked up to him and then back toward the keep. "I was told by the guards at the gate that they keep watch on the shoreline." She studied him, her gaze traveling down his chest to his waist. "Ye have no weapon yerself."

He gave her a droll look. "If ye were to be attacked here, and the guards had the eyes of a hawk, how long before they could reach ye?"

Chin lifted defiantly, he could tell she'd not acquiesce. "Do ye believe those men, who've been attacking people would dare to come here within the sight of Keep Ross?"

They wouldn't, but that wasn't the point he wished to make. "Why is someone nae with ye?"

"Yer mother is resting. Ainslie is feeling poorly. And I dinnae know any of the servants well enough to ask one to walk with me."

He doubted a small detail like that would keep Nala from asking for someone to come with her. She liked time alone. He understood it.

When he looked at her, she was studying him, searching his face. For what he wasn't sure. But when his body began to react, he eyed the water. "Let us walk back."

Nala stood her ground. She turned to look at the ocean and closed her eyes. Tears slid down her cheeks and she sniffed.

After hesitating, he placed a hand on her shoulder, hating that she trembled. This was a side of Nala, he wasn't sure how to deal with. "Nala, why are ye crying?"

Keeping her attention on the horizon, she swallowed and took a breath. "I feel as if I have little say in my circumstances."

"If given a choice what would ye want to do with yer life?"

Eyes wet, she looked up at him. Even with her nose pink and lashes clumped from crying, she was amazingly beautiful.

"I-I am nae sure. No one has ever asked me."

When she fell against him, seeming exhausted, Alexander wrapped his arms around her. "Ye wish to ken what I think?" he whispered into her ear. "If ye marry the right man, ye will have many of the same freedoms ye have now."

She shuddered and let out a long breath, her head on his chest. He tipped her chin up and met her gaze. "I will do what I can to ensure ye are well taken care of."

When Nala's gaze lingered on his lips, he was lost to her.

All thought left except the need to kiss her, and Alexander took her mouth reveling in the feel of her taste. When her arms wrapped around him and she responded, time stood still.

Attackers could have approached, and Alexander would have been helpless because, in that moment, only Nala existed. He plundered her mouth, slipping his tongue between her lips and she melted against him. Her fingers digging into his back pulling him closer.

The hardening of his shaft brought Alexander out of the whirlwind that was the beauty in his arms, and he pulled back.

They were breathless, chests heaving, eyes locked.

"I-I..." Nala began, pressing her hand over her mouth.

"I apologize," Alexander said motioning for her to walk ahead, he didn't dare touch her for fear he wouldn't be able to pull away again. "We should head back."

As they walked back, Nala gave him a questioning look, her swollen lips beckoning for another kiss. "Ye dinnae have to apologize." The fiery lass lifted a brow. "I quite enjoyed it."

Fighting the urge to puff out his chest, Alexander pressed his lips together to contain a smile. "I am glad to hear it."

"Dinnae do it again," Nala quipped. "Or I will demand ye marry me."

"What?" Alexander stopped in his tracks. "Why?"

Nala gave him a droll look and continued walking. "I jest. However, it would nae be a bad idea. Neither of us wish to marry. We can pretend."

Alexander raked hair away from his face. She was so beautiful it took his breath away. It was easy to imagine a life with her. "When I marry it will be someone willing to be my wife in every aspect. Someone I care for and who cares for me."

Her mouth fell open and then closed, gathering her skirts, she walked faster, trying to get away from him. They'd arrived back at the lower portion of the keep, from which they'd have to climb stairs to get to the main house.

When Alexander caught up to her and took her arm, she'd climbed a pair of steps so that they were at eye level when she turned and he asked, "Are ye cross?"

She bit her bottom lip catching his attention and reminding Alexander that he'd had the morsel in his mouth. "Ye would never marry me. That is what ye mean to say."

"I didnae say that."

Nala let out a huff. "Good because I would never marry ye." With that, she took her skirts with both hands and ran up the steps.

Alexander scratched his nape. Women were confusing creatures.

CHAPTER SEVEN

Nala watched through the parlor window as Alexander mounted and rode out past the gates. Immediately her mind went to the day before. Thoughts of his hard body against hers, his arms surrounding her like a protective cloak.

Of their own accord, her eyes fluttered shut and she touched the tips of her fingers to her lips.

He was alone. A dangerous thing to do. As laird, he was a prime target for anyone wishing to do damage to Clan Ross. Perhaps she'd bring it up to him.

Moments later, two guards rode out at a gallop toward where Alexander went. Obviously, others noticed that he'd left.

Still touching her lips, she kept watch, her mind still reeling from being with Alexander on the shore. It was most perplexing that he'd acted as if nothing happened after they'd kissed. It could be because kissing a lass was nothing new to him. Women probably flocked to him, and he had his choice of who to be with.

Just the thought of Alexander's mouth on another woman's made her bristle. Stupid reaction. He didn't belong to anyone and certainly not her. She'd made it abundantly clear she was not going into marriage willingly.

Had he kissed her to prove a point? That she could be

swayed into reacting to a man's touch?

Nala supposed if that was to be his point, it had succeeded. Her entire body had responded to him. Alexander was nothing like the young men she'd flirted with in London. Their kisses had been tepid at best. Never once had a kiss consumed her like it had with Alexander.

He was nothing like the slender, pampered men she'd known most of her life. Instead, he was the total opposite. Rugged, muscular, powerful, and dangerous. For a moment, when they'd been kissing and she'd held him, he'd given himself to her. He had responded to her touch, if the soft moans he was making while they were kissing were anything to go by.

In that moment she'd felt as powerful as him.

Then she'd suggested they marry. It was mortifying to recall it. Even as the words left her mouth, she'd wished the ground would have swallowed her up.

He wanted a wife that would be fully his. Body and soul.

He'd not rejected her, Nala supposed. He'd rejected the idea of what she'd proposed. Besides, it was expected of him to marry for the benefit of the clan. She'd bring little benefit. Yes, her father was wealthy, but so was Alexander. Her family didn't possess great stables, nor did they have a guard force that could join Clan Ross'.

"There ye are," Ainslie walked into the room looking refreshed and carrying a large basket overspilling with what looked to be linens of some sort.

Glad for the distraction, Nala walked to where Ainslie had settled into a chair and placed the basket on the floor. "What are ye doing with those?"

"Tear them into strips for bandages," Ainslie replied with a shake of her head. "After the MacLeod attacks, we ran out."

"I will help ye," Nala said and lowered to a chair opposite. "Mother and I usually tear something if someone is injured. I will suggest we have some prepared ahead of time."

"I saw ye return from outside yesterday, ye seemed upset. Yer face was flushed," Ainslie said.

"I went for a walk along the seashore until Alexander scolded me for walking too far." Nala kept her gaze lowered. Just the thought of the seashore made her heart quicken.

Ainslie chuckled. "He takes the responsibility of yer well-being seriously. Yer father trusted him with ye."

"The main thing Father and Mother wish for is for Alexander to find me a husband. I wish they'd allow me to choose if I wish to marry or nae." Nala hated the petulant tone she'd spoken in, but at the same time, she was not happy at the current turn of events.

Ainslie nodded in agreement. "Sometimes we are fortunate and find a love match. Have ye considered finding a husband yerself and not waiting for someone else to decide?"

Unfortunately, the only man who formed in her mind was Alexander and Nala let out a sharp breath. "Who, of the men here, would ye consider if ye were nae married to Cynden?"

A smile crept up at Ainslie's happy expression. "I have nae considered it. Let me think. What about Knox? He is bonny. Then there is Hendry… a bit rugged, but handsome."

Nala pictured both men and had to agree, both were good candidates. "What of their temperament? Would they be strict with me?"

"Of the two, Hendry has an even temperament. I have nae

seen him ever lose his temper. Knox, I would describe as stubborn and a bit of a rogue."

"A bit?" Nala asked as she tore a cloth in half. "He is a rogue. I've heard about his many conquests. The only one I know has resisted him, is my dear friend, Sencha."

"Hmm." Ainslie tapped a finger to her chin as if in thought. "Aye, Knox would nae be a good husband. He has nae settled."

"So Hendry it is," Nala said. "I will find and speak to him. If he is agreeable. I will ask that he marry me. Then it will be done and over with."

There were several beats of silence and Nala looked up from her task at Ainslie, who stared at her slack jawed.

"He will expect his rights as a husband. Are ye prepared for it?" Ainslie asked, looking skeptical.

"I dinnae ken as yet, perhaps if I spend some time with him. 'Tis better than awaiting fate and having no say," Nala stated, not sure if Ainslie was breathing. "Is something wrong?"

Ainslie let out a breath. "I can help ye. But are ye sure? Is there no one else that catches yer fancy? That ye would possibly fall in love with?"

Again the only man who she pictured was Alexander. It was Nala's turn to let out a breath. "Aye, there is someone, but he would never marry me. It is only recently that I discovered I have deep feelings for him."

"Alexander," Ainslie said, shocking Nala.

"Why would ye say that?"

Her companion laughed. "Because the pull between the two of ye is obvious. At least to me it is. Neither of ye can keep from glancing at each other. Just yesterday at last meal, Lady Ross and I began to count how many times ye both exchanged glances."

Heat rose up from her neck. It felt as if she held her face too close to fire. How was it possible that others could see what she had not? It could be that she kept looking to him out of curiosity. Puzzled and surprised by the many sides to him. If he had kept an eye on her, it was out of the responsibility he felt.

"I dinnae…" Nala started, then began again. "It matters not. His duty to the clan dictates who he marries. I am nae in contention."

"Look around," Ainslie said, holding her arms wide. "Are there any other women who would be?"

Mentally, she pictured the people in the great room, those who came to seek the laird and others who visited. There had been several unmarried women, but they'd been villagers.

"I will speak to Hendry. If he is back from patrol," Nala insisted stubbornly.

"Two and Ten," Ainslie said with a pointed look.

"What?" Nala looked down at the bandages, she'd not been counting.

Ainslie smiled. "The times we counted ye and Alexander looking to one another. At least those were the times we caught it."

IT WAS THE next day and Nala had yet to find the opportunity to speak to Hendry. She'd taken extra care with her hair and dress that morning before attending first meal. The warrior was at a table surrounded by guards, and she'd dared not approach. He'd not once looked in her direction, which was troubling.

Taking advantage of her viewpoint, she studied him. Hendry was indeed attractive. A complete contrast to Alexander. Hendry had light brown hair that fell to his broad shoulders and bright blue eyes. The bottom half of his features were covered with a trimmed beard and mustache that suited him.

Unlike many of the others, he ate slowly and with care not to spill food. That was something, Nala supposed.

"Studying yer prey?" Ainslie whispered and Nala smiled widely.

"Aye, I am."

"Do ye require assistance getting him away from the others?" Apparently, Ainslie had appointed herself as her cohort in the endeavor.

Nala's eyes narrowed. "How would ye do it?"

"No one will suspect a thing."

Ainslie waited until Hendry finished eating and went to him as he stood. She said something to him, and he nodded. Then both came to where Nala sat.

"Miss Nala," he said. "I am Hendry. Miss Ainslie said ye wish to find a docile horse to ride?"

"Oh…" Caught off guard, Nala tried to think of a suitable reply. The last thing she'd wish for was a docile horse. "Aye. A horse. Not too docile."

"I dinnae have patrol until midday. I can escort ye on a ride if ye wish." His expression was set, it was impossible to guess what he thought.

Purposely, Nala looked directly into his eyes to see how he'd react. Hendry slid a look to Ainslie and then back to her. "Is something wrong, miss?"

"Call me Nala, please," she said. "Allow me to change my skirts. I will be down shortly."

As she walked from the room, Nala didn't look in Alexander's direction but sensed him watching. When she returned moments later wearing a riding skirt, she caught a glimpse of him out of the corner of her eyes. He openly watched her as she went to Hendry, who stood in the doorway.

Unable to keep from it as she walked with Hendry, Nala stole a look toward the high board. Alexander continued to watch, and from the way his eyes narrowed he wondered what she was up to.

Did he think she tried to get away? If she did, the last thing she'd ask was for a Ross guard to escort her.

Upon reaching the stables, Hendry asked her to remain by the fence as he hurried away. It wasn't much longer that he returned with two horses, both saddled.

To her surprise, the horse he'd chosen was almost as powerful as his.

"Do ye require assistance mounting?" Hendry asked.

Normally Nala did not, but she decided it was an opportunity for proximity. "Please."

Nala expected he'd cup his hands for her to step up and onto the saddle. Instead, he looked from her to the horse and without hesitation took Nala by the waist and lifted her to the saddle. Nala expertly straddled the horse.

She looked to Hendry, but he was looking away. This was going to prove annoying if the man paid her little to no mind.

When he mounted, he looked over at her. "Seashore or fields?"

"Fields," she replied, excited to be on horseback again.

They rode at a leisurely pace, and Hendry didn't seem to mind the silence between them. It was as if his mind were elsewhere. The whole time they rode, he kept scanning the area, keeping watch.

After an hour or so, Nala turned to him. "Does yer family live nearby?"

He nodded and pointed toward the west. "Not too far from the village. My parents and two sisters."

"How long have ye worked for the laird?"

His lips curved softening his rugged features. "I have been friends with the Ross brothers since a wee lad. It was never questioned that I would work at the keep. First, I worked in the kitchens and then as a stable lad. Finally, I trained to become a warrior."

"Ye have always known yer destiny then?" Nala said more than asked.

Hendry slid his gaze to her. "Most of us do I think."

"Mine is dictated by my father. To marry and become a wife and mother." She turned to study the open fields. Tall grasses swayed in the wind and the leaves on trees fluttered as if dancing. Sheep grazed, their tails swishing side to side on sloping hills. In the distance there was a cottage where she assumed the caretakers lived.

"'Tis nae a bad life." Hendry followed her line of vision. "I wish to marry one day, sire bairns, and live in a cottage like that one. Care for my wife, my family, my land. And nae fight anymore."

The admission took Nala by surprise. "Ye would leave the guard?"

He shrugged. "Aye, I cannae be a warrior forever. It is the role of the fit and young." Pulling his horse short, he motioned for her to do the same. Then he turned to a grouping of trees, and she followed.

"It may be nothing, but I caught sight of riders," Hendry said in a low voice.

Moments later, in the distance, a group of five men rode down a path toward the seashore. They would not come near where they hid.

Hendry leaned forward over his horse watching the men intently. "Do they look familiar to ye?" he asked.

Like him, Nala also tracked the group. One of the men was familiar. He'd been with those who'd attacked the couple in the wagon. But she couldn't admit it. "Nae. I have never seen any of them before."

"Where are they headed?" Hendry said, more to himself than her.

"We can follow them," Nala suggested.

Her companion shook his head. "Nae. If they are the attackers, I will nae put ye in danger."

If only she'd thought to bring her bow. Instead, she'd been hoping to find commonalities with Hendry and find out if a connection with him could be made.

It had not worked. The man had been distracted the entire time. Keeping an eye out for possible danger. He was working, not out for a leisurely ride.

"We must return." Without waiting for her reply, he turned his horse around and they galloped back to the keep.

Once back in the courtyard, he helped her down, once again taking her by the waist. Hendry handed the reins to stable lads giving instructions not to unsaddle his horse.

"Thank ye," Nala said to his retreating back as he hurried into the house.

She remained in the courtyard, wondering what had been accomplished. Other than spotting the attackers, which was a good thing, nothing had formed between her and Hendry.

Moments later, swords strapped to their back, four warriors rushed out of the house. Hendry, along with Alexander and two others.

As he walked past, Alexander glowered in her direction. It was as if he was furious at her.

Nala let out a huff. Whatever was his reason for being cross? If not for her asking to go on a ride with Hendry, they'd not know which direction to go in hope of possibly finding the attackers.

By the time the group rode out from the keep, another four men had joined them.

Nala wondered why they didn't take more.

Her question was answered when, yet another group of warriors rushed to the stables and once mounted followed after Alexander's group.

Closing her eyes, she said a silent prayer, asking for their safe return. She would be devasted if anything happened to Alexander.

The warriors soon disappeared from sight, but she knew all would be well. Not only would the attackers be outnumbered, but also, the Ross warriors were well trained in battle.

CHAPTER EIGHT

ALEXANDER PRAYED THEY'D find the men, question them, and finally put an end to the senseless attacks on his clan. It was time for peace. For the people to be able to live without fear. Frankly he grew tired of the constant strife that never seemed to end. First the Mackinnons, then the attacks from the MacLeods, followed by the renegade attackers who sought nothing more than discord and fear.

If the attackers had continued in the direction Hendry had seen them going, they went toward an area that wasn't part of Clan Ross lands, which made little sense.

The lands past a narrow river belonged to Clan Grant, an ally of Clan Ross. Alexander would have to pay the laird a visit and find out if that clan had also been victimized, or if they'd been harboring the attackers.

Following Hendry's directions, they soon neared the northwestern shoreline. There was a thick forested area blocking the view. On the lands surrounding the trees, there was nothing in sight. It was possible the attackers had either left or hid.

Silently, Alexander motioned for half of the men to go to his right while he and the others went left. With twenty men, it would be impossible for a group of five to avoid being caught if they remained in the area.

Riding into the trees, they moved without speaking, everyone listening for any suspicious noises. Knox was on foot, pulling his horse behind as he tracked for any signs of others going before them.

Another tracker had gone with the other group to do the same.

His body was on full alert, every muscle tensed and ready for a fight. Alexander sensed they were close and would soon find the attackers. The question was, how should it be handled?

The council had suggested the men be apprehended and brought before the people to be punished. It would not only be a warning to any others who rode with them, but also give the clan reassurance that Alexander had indeed fought for their safety.

They'd almost surrounded the wooded area when the screams tore through the trees from the direction of the other group. His group remained in their section continuing forward effectively blocking the way toward Mackinnon lands. If any of the five tried to escape they would be caught.

Alexander held up a hand. "Hold steady and wait."

Moments later two horsemen appeared. By the time they noticed Alexander and his men, it was too late to retreat.

Instead of surrendering, the idiots charged forward swinging their swords.

"Aim to injure, not kill," Alexander instructed as one of the men closed in. He deflected each strike of the man's sword.

"Give yerself up," he yelled.

The man acted as if deranged, yelling whilst continuing to attack. "Ye deserve death," he yelled. "Ye and yers killed my brother and father."

"In battle," Alexander replied once again blocking the man's downward momentum. "Ye and yers are attacking innocents."

When the man thrust his sword forward in an attempt to stab Alexander, he evaded the strike and swung his weapon sideways. It sliced into the man's arm, cutting through flesh and muscle.

The man whirled his horse around only to see that he was surrounded by warriors.

Alexander motioned for his men to remain in place.

Just then the other man slumped down atop his horse, either gravely injured or dead.

At noticing, Alexander's opponent let out an angry growl and with his sword lifted he charged in Alex's direction. "I may die, but there are others who will continue to avenge—" He stopped speaking when an arrow sunk into his sword arm.

The man yelped in pain as his sword dropped to the ground.

Alexander lifted his sword and pressed it to the man's throat. "Ye are my prisoner now."

Glancing over at the one slumped over his horse, he asked. "Is that one dead?"

One of the guards held a hand over a cut on his side. "He would nae stop." The warrior frowned. "Apologies, Laird."

There was nothing that could be done about it, so Alexander shrugged.

"Tie him up," Alexander ordered motioning to the man he held at bay.

When the man tried to reach for something, probably a

dirk in his boot, his left arm flopped uselessly at his side. It was then he seemed to notice the deep cut for the first time. Blood dripped down his arm and onto the ground. There was little he could do to staunch the flow, as the other arm had an arrow through it.

He glared at Alexander. "I wish ye were dead."

Alexander met his gaze. "And yet I am nae. Ye will die and yer death will serve as a warning to others."

Something akin to fear flashed in the man's eyes before he was led away.

THEY EMERGED FROM the woods with their prisoner and moments later the other party emerged with two others.

Alexander weighed the options regarding what was best to do with their prisoners. Finally, he decided they would be taken to the Clan's people.

"Take them to Tokavaig, to the village square. They will be executed in the morn." He motioned to Hendry. "Go with ten men."

After instructing a group of guards to return to the woods and bury the dead man, he and Knox rode back to the keep with the last of the contingency.

"I believe that was the last of them," Alexander said to his cousin. "It has to be."

"Aye, I agree," Knox replied. "It makes sense. From what we've seen and heard, there were never more than four or five attackers at once. One was killed. I believe these men were the last of them."

They rode for a while longer, Alexander noticing a gash on his left forearm. At his notice the injury began to throb. He gritted his teeth in annoyance. Hopefully it would be the last of his battle wounds for a long time.

"Once this is dealt with, I plan to visit the Grant," Alexander said to Knox. "There had to be a reason why they were headed there."

Knox nodded. "I wondered the same thing. Unless they planned to attack a different clan. But it makes little sense."

"Clan Grant battled with the late Mackinnon, but that was a long time ago," Alexander commented. "It makes little sense that they would attack Clan Grant, but then again, they are all mad."

Knox let out a snort and shook his head. "A small group of renegades against two lairds. They must have a death wish."

"Then it is about to come true," Alexander said. His people would be satisfied. Even though it was never a good day when a life was taken, at the same time, it was the only way to ensure not only peace for his clan but give his people the reassurance they needed.

They were met with cheers upon arriving back at the keep. Alexander gave his cousin a droll look. "We fought against men, who were nae well trained. I would nae call it a huge victory."

"A win is a win," Knox replied holding his arms up and joining in the celebration by letting out a battle cry.

One thing about Knox. There was little that dampened the man's spirit. Alexander grinned when Knox made his horse turn in circles, the whole time singing a victory song.

Those inside the house came out at the commotion and joined in the celebration. It was a good day for Clan Ross, and he was glad to see the expressions of happiness on his people's faces.

His mother appeared in the doorway and looked to him. With a proud expression, she met his gaze and crossed both hands over her chest. It was something she'd done ever since he could remember. Upon his father's return from battle and now when he and his brothers returned victorious their mother would greet them with a proud stance, hands over her chest.

Alexander's heart swelled with pride.

Ainslie rushed out tugging Nala behind. They were joined by several maids, and they all clasped hands and danced in a circle. It was a beautiful sight seeing Nala so carefree, a bright smile on her face as she skipped in time with the others.

He climbed the steps to the front entrance. His mother cupped his face and kissed his cheeks. "Today ye make our clan proud. Ye are a leader of great worth my son."

Tears sprung to his eyes, and he had to blink them back. When he tried to speak, words would not come.

His mother smiled up at him seeming to understand. "I will have a feast prepared and this day we shall celebrate."

Last meal was indeed a celebration. A huge bonfire blazed, lighting up the night. Musicians played lively tunes and people, their spirits lifted by the many pitchers of ale and mead, danced gaily.

On long tables, others partook of the offerings. Platters were heaped with roasted pig, hens, breads, and cheeses.

Alexander did his best not to imbibe too much, but after

being pulled into a dance several times, he required a cool ale.

"Dance with Nala," Ainslie said pulling at his tartan sleeve. "Ye have danced with every lass but her."

He drank deeply from the tankard. "I am nae sure I'm able to dance. I have had too much ale."

"Nonsense," Ainslie insisted. "Go now. I told her ye would dance with her."

He frowned at his brother's wife. "What are ye up to?"

"Nothing at all. Making sure ye dinnae slight our guest." Ainslie took his tankard. "Go."

He'd hoped to sneak off to bed as it would be very early the next morning that they were all to leave for Tokavaig.

Walking across the space between him and Ainslie, someone pulled at his arm. It was a lass he'd already danced with. "Dance with me, Laird," she said, her eyes met his and moved to his mouth. "I will repay ye fully."

The proposition was obvious and yet, it didn't interest him as it would have in the past. "I must dance with my guest." He disengaged from the woman and continued to where Nala was.

From Alexander's right Hendry appeared. He headed toward Nala. What was he doing there? He'd sent him off to the village.

Alexander walked fast, reaching Nala a few steps ahead of Hendry. The warrior continued past, not seeming to notice. Perhaps he'd not been going toward Nala.

"A dance?" he said holding his hand out.

"Aye, of course."

Holding Nala by the hand, they joined a lively dance, which admittedly, he wasn't the best at. The inability to keep up and potentially looking clumsy was worth it because of the joyful expression on Nala's face. Lips curved and sparkly eyes, she beamed happily as she circled around him. There was a playful, flirty expression when she looked up at him that made something flutter in his gut.

Alexander couldn't tear his eyes from her as they made their way toward the center, when it was their turn to be circled. They held hands and spun as the other dancers began to whirl around them, surrounding them with a ring of laughter and music.

If it were possible to remain in that moment longer, Alexander would have thanked God. For the first time since he could remember, everything outside the circle of dancers, all the problems, situations, and responsibilities seemed to be swept away. There was only him and the beautiful woman who looked up at him with what he could only call coyness.

He met her gaze wishing that they were alone so that he could take her into his arms and kiss her once again. Nala's lips curved almost as if she read his mind. When her gaze drifted down to his mouth, it was obvious she too was recalling their moment at the seashore.

When laughter erupted nearby, he realized the music had stopped. Nala blinked. "Oh. I supposed the song has ended."

"Aye, it has." Alexander took her hand and led her toward where she'd been standing. "Ye look beautiful tonight, Nala."

For a moment, he thought she'd not heard him, but then she glanced up at him. "It could be the ale speaking."

"Walk with me." He guided her away from the others, so they could look out to the sea.

When she shivered, he placed an arm around her shoulders. "Are ye cold?"

Nala shook her head. "The breeze feels wonderful on my overheated face." Facing the sky, she closed her eyes and let out a long breath. "It is wonderful that peace has finally come to the isle."

"Aye, it is." He couldn't look away. Nala was like a magical creature who enraptured him. It wasn't often that he'd felt helpless when near a woman. If ever there was a time that he was so drawn to another, he couldn't remember.

"Nala," he said about to propose they walk back to the festivities. It was late and he planned to retire.

"Mmm?" she murmured.

"It is late."

When she looked at him, the corners of her mouth lifted just enough. She looked like a satisfied kitten. "I agree. I will remain here just a bit longer, then I will seek my bed."

Alexander lingered, feeling like a lad of ten and five, attempting to find a way to ask for a kiss. He was laird of the clan and here he stood like a tongue-tied idiot.

"Sleep well," he finally managed.

The softness of her hand in his sent a shiver of awareness up his arm. Nala held it for a moment. "Thank ye for dancing with me. I enjoyed it."

If he didn't kiss her now, he would regret it. Alexander bent until their faces were a hair's breadth apart. "The pleasure was all mine." Then he kissed her. Not an all-consuming kiss, as they were not far from the celebration, and it was possible they'd be seen. Instead, he kept himself from touching her, allowing his lips to linger over hers for a bit longer than he should have. Then he straightened.

"Sleep well, Laird," Nala said turning to once again look out to the sea with a soft expression.

He almost asked if the kiss was not to her liking but decided that it was. Or was it?

Annoyed at himself for even questioning his kissing skills, Alexander stalked away.

"Ye kissed her," Ainslie said by way of greeting as he entered the house. She clapped her hands and gave a delighted squeal. "Good on ye."

"What are ye going on about?" Cynden came to stand next to his wife, his hazel gaze moving from her to Alexander.

Before Alexander could say anything Ainslie spoke. "Alexander danced with and then kissed the beautiful Nala." Ainslie grinned widely. "It could be the both of them finally accept they are smitten with each other."

Cynden's eyebrows lifted higher than Alexander thought possible. "Is that true Alex?"

"I am going to seek my bed. We leave at daylight." He walked to the stairwell. "Ensure the guardsmen are ready."

"Ye can wait until after first meal." His mother walked in from outside, her face flushed as if she'd just walked straight inside after dancing. She fanned her face with both hands. "What a delightful day."

"There is much to do tomorrow," Alexander insisted.

His mother gave him a pointed look. "'Tis better to allow the men to sleep a bit. Yerself as well. Riding out with heavy heads and slack gut will nae do anyone a bit of good."

She breezed up the stairs past him. "I will see ye at first meal, son."

THE ATTACKERS CAPTURED had been hanged by the neck until dead. Two of the men had accepted their fates with defiance, screaming obscenities at the guards and promising that their deaths would be avenged. One man was not as willing to face death. He'd pleaded and begged that his life be spared, calling out that he was the only provider for his wife and bairns. The man had wailed up until the rope had been placed over his head. Then he'd fainted. It had been a reprieve, Alexander considered.

As heartbreaking as it was to take a man's life who had a wife and children, he had to consider that the man had been part of a group who had killed Edgar, a man who also had a wife and bairns.

Said woman was present. Surrounded by her parents and her children, she'd yelled out her husband's name, repeating over and over that they'd killed her husband and father of her bairns.

Alexander, his mother, and his brothers, Cynden and Munro, stood out on the tavern's second-story balcony that overlooked the village square. From there he kept watch over the proceedings.

His mother had hidden her face only once. During the first hanging. After that she'd remained strong, her gaze ahead. Whether she watched or not, he wasn't sure, but she understood how important her presence was for the people.

As the laden wagon rolled away, people threw rocks at the bodies until they were out of reach. After the crowd dissipated, everyone returned to their homes or to work. Life would continue for the clan's people, but at least now they felt safe from the random attacks.

The bodies of the dead men were placed onto the back of a wagon. Escorted by a contingency of warriors, they would be delivered to Armandale and left at the village square there. Alexander hoped it would send a message that anyone who came against Clan Ross and attacked his clan's people would meet the same fate.

"Where is Ainslie?" Munro asked Cynden.

Cynden shook his head. "Neither she nor Nala wished to come. Ainslie is sensitive and I understand, and Nala wished to keep her company."

"Aye, Lila would nae come either," Munro said, referring to his wife. "Nala?" he asked, a smile curving his lips. "The wee Nala has come back."

"Aye, and she is nae wee. But a beauty now," Cynden replied. Looking to Alexander, he added. "Do ye nae think so Alex?"

His brothers and mother looked to him, and Alex shrugged as if it was nothing of importance. "Aye, the lass is bonny."

"A lovely creature she is," his mother added. "Ye and Lila should come visit soon. Nala is staying with us as our guest."

"Alex is to find her a husband," Cynden, ever helpful, added.

"What about Knox?" Munro asked.

Why was Knox the first one everyone seemed to think was the best option for Nala? Not that he wished to marry, and yet for whatever reason Alexander found it off-putting.

Cynden leaned forward and spoke in a whisper. "It could be the lass has gotten the attention of someone else."

"Who?" Alexander asked, then caught himself. "I mean, it could be this man is nae a suitable match for the lass."

His mother nodded. "I think he is. A perfect match if ye were to ask me."

Munro nodded knowingly. "I am inclined to agree."

Alexander's stomach plummeted and he inhaled to keep from flinching. Why did the idea of the lass marrying a suitable man affect him so? Aye, he was man enough to admit he found her appealing. But it was a passing fancy. Surely, it was nothing more.

"Let us go," Cynden said. "They bring the coach and our horses."

As they walked down the stairwell in the tavern, Alexander tapped Cynden's shoulder. His brother could barely turn in the narrow passage. Both of their shoulders were almost as wide. Munro had to turn a bit sideways to fit through.

"Who is it?"

Cynden gave him a droll look. "Do ye really have to ask? Ye are daft."

"Ye are the daft one," Alexander retorted, then realized they'd returned to their youth. "The only reason I ask is because I was charged by her father to find a proper husband. Not some fool who can only offer that he is besotted with her."

At Cynden's chuckling, he fought the urge to kick his brother. "They are talking about ye, ye daft idiot."

Alexander frowned. "Me?" He fought the urge to smile. "Ye are the idiot. It is nae me they speak of."

They made their way to the main room of the tavern and

the owner approached. "Thank ye, Laird. For everything. We are ever thankful for the ability to travel freely on our home isle."

More people approached as they made their way through, calling out their appreciation, declaring they'd never lost faith in him.

Munro gave him a knowing look. Both were lairds and knew that the very same people would be defiant and declare them unsuitable at the first sign of trouble.

His mother slipped her arm through his. "Let us return home. There is much to do."

CHAPTER NINE

THE SUN CAME through her bedchamber's window and Nala stretched. She'd been sitting on the floor folding her newly dried garments. She stood, opened the trunk she'd brought with her and placed the items into it with care.

Greetings from the guards carried upward, and she went to the window. The Ross family along with a contingency of warriors arrived. Beside the coach, was Alexander, his black hair shimmering in the sunlight making it seem otherworldly. Just behind the carriage rode Cynden and another man. She squinted at the newcomer, not quite sure who he was.

The man was broad and muscular with the same color hair as Cynden. He wore a beard and across his wide shoulders the Clan Ross tartan. A member of the family. She would find out soon enough, Nala figured.

Then a thought crossed her mind. Was he being brought as a potential husband for her? Surely not. They had more pressing matters at the moment. It was doubtful that while watching an execution, Alexander would be so cavalier as to play matchmaker.

Curiosity got the best of her. Standing, she smoothed her skirts then unbraided her hair. After brushing it, she braided it again, with expert fingers. Once the task was done, she pinned her hair up and pulled curls down to frame her face.

From the bedchamber, she peered into Cynden and Ainslie's room, it was empty. So she hurried down the stairs and to the parlor hoping to find Ainslie there, but the woman was nowhere to be found.

Finally, she went to the great room, it too was empty. Everyone was probably in the courtyard to welcome the laird back. At the front door, she found Ainslie holding a handkerchief to her eyes.

"What is the matter?" Nala asked taking her friend by the shoulders. "Did something happen?"

Ainslie shook her head. "I dinnae ken why I am so weepy today. It is terribly sad that those men had to die. Is it not?"

"It is," Nala replied. "Ye must remember, they killed others and had to be punished. They knew what would happen if caught."

"I do understand," Ainslie replied with a shaky breath. "I tire of it. The senseless deaths."

Nala understood her friend. Ainslie was with child, and it tended to make women weepy. At least that was what her mother had told her.

Just then Cynden walked in. His eyes widened at seeing his wife's stricken face and he rushed to her. "Is something wrong?" The warrior took her into his arms, his handsome face pale.

When he met Nala's gaze, she gave him what she hoped was a reassuring smile. "Ainslie is sad that the men had to be executed."

"Do ye wish for some sweet mead?" he asked gently. Ainslie sniffed and nodded. The warrior lifted his woman up in his arms and carried her to the stairs.

Nala watched them and wondered if she'd ever find a man who would care for her as deeply.

"Nala," Alexander's deep voice startled her, and she whirled to see him standing next to the muscular man. "Do ye ken who this is?"

Swallowing past the dryness in her throat, Nala looked from Alexander to the other man, who watched her with interest, a warm expression on his ruggedly handsome face.

"Munro!" Nala threw herself at the warrior, lifting to her toes and pressing kisses to his cheeks. "Ye look so very different. Ye are huge."

Thick arms wrapped around her, and he lifted her off her feet then twirled in a circle, his rich laughter loud in her ears.

He placed her down with a gentleness that was surprising, then cupped her face, his green gaze taking her in. "Alex told me ye had become a beautiful woman. He didnae do ye justice. Other than my wife, a more beautiful woman I have never seen."

"Oh, aye," Nala said smiling widely. "Ye married a woman called Lila. Mother told me all about it. She and I planned to visit, but with all the attacks, it was too dangerous."

Munro kissed her brow. "I have missed ye, lass."

Too happy for words, she clung to Munro's arm as they made their way into the great room. "Ye must sit with me and talk once ye rest. I wish to hear all that ye have done since I left Skye."

His hearty laughter made Nala join in. "It would take long a tale to tell ye what occurred over the years ye were gone, lass," he stated.

People began streaming into the great room. Some were

guests who'd come to witness the executions. They'd be there to eat and rest before continuing on to their destinations. Others, like her parents, came to show appreciation to Alexander.

Nala went to her mother, and they embraced. "I didnae ken ye would be here today." She motioned to Munro, who'd joined the others at the high board. "It is Munro."

Her mother nodded. "I ken dear. I have seen him several times since ye left." Her mother chuckled. "He is a gentle man for being so… big." They giggled as they made their way to where Lady Ross sat.

DURING THE MEAL, Nala noted that Alexander was solemn. She supposed watching an execution was not something that lifted yer spirits. Yet, Lady Ross and the others didn't seem as affected.

When he walked from the room, Nala excused herself and followed him at a distance.

He walked down a short corridor, past his study then down another corridor. Nala had not been in that area of the keep, the corridor was dim and foreboding.

When Alexander hesitated near a door, Nala ducked into a hollow in the wall and waited a beat before peering out to see what he did. Alexander opened the door and walked into a room.

Nala strained to listen for any sounds, but it was silent. Finally, on tiptoes, she closed the distance between her hiding place and the room, the whole time keeping an ear out for any sounds.

Upon coming to the doorway, she peeked inside through

the open door.

It seemed to be a healer's depository. A shelf holding jars of different sizes lined one wall. In the center was a narrow table, upon which rested scales, a mortar and pestle, and an array of tools such as knives, scissors, needles, and shallow bowls.

Through a small window, a bit of sunlight lit the room enough to see. Alexander pushed the shutter open wider and stood looking out, hands to his sides, still as a statue.

Nala watched him for a long moment, noting his powerful build and strong stance. He never seemed to relax, to allow himself moments of vulnerability.

Then he did. His shoulders rounded and he lifted his hands to cover his face. Alexander kept his head bowed, not making a sound. She wondered if he cried or prayed. Either way, it was not her place to intrude when he obviously sought to be alone.

She took a step backward, her shoe sliding against the stone floor. Nala froze. The sound, although soft, caught Alexander's attention and he turned, his red-rimmed eyes looked at her then he turned away without a word.

There were two choices. Stay and comfort him or leave him to his thoughts.

Nala turned away, but then she heard a long sigh, and it broke her heart. She walked to where he stood, came up behind him, and wrapped her arms around his midsection.

"I am here. Ye dinnae have to talk to me."

He sagged against her, his large frame heavy, but Nala didn't mind. The ten years they'd been apart melted, and it was as if they'd always been together. He wasn't just a strong formidable man, but he was her friend, her protector, the man whom she trusted more than anyone.

Alexander turned and she dropped her arms.

"If ye need to be alone…" Nala began.

He shook his head and took her hand leading her to a chair. Lowering to sit, he pulled Nala onto his lap and then hugged her tightly. "I am tired. That is all."

To her it seemed there was more to it. That something weighed so heavily, he could not bear it. "Today was hard for ye. I cannae imagine having to order the execution of men, no matter their sins."

Nala kept her voice even. "Ye did the right thing, Alex."

It was the first time she'd called him by name. Nala couldn't suppress the sweet feeling at how easily it had come to her lips.

In the depths of his eyes, she saw a storm. "A man pleaded for his life. Cried out that he had a wife and bairns. I almost ordered him to be released."

"People will say many things when pleading for their lives," Nala said.

Alexander continued, "Said he'd never taken part in any of the attacks. That he was nae involved. What if he told the truth?"

The fact he was laird meant Alexander could never show any remorse or doubts about orders given, especially at a time when the clan's people needed him to be at his strongest. They needed a leader who defended them at all costs. Without doubting himself. It was the only way to earn the respect and loyalty of his clan.

Nala cupped his face with both hands, the shading of his

beard prickly in her palms. If not for the need to be strong for him, she would have acknowledged how much she wanted to kiss him.

"What if he lied? Ye can ask questions about it until the end of time. What we do ken is that the men he rode with killed without mercy. Ignored the pleas of the people they slaughtered. What of that man Edgar? That he had a family didnae spare his life. Aye, perhaps this man never took part, but he knew them and knew what they did. That he kept silent meant he did take part."

The corners of Alexander's lips twitched. "When did ye become so wise, lass?"

Warmth heated her cheeks, and she looked away. "I am nae wise."

"Ye called me Alex," he pressed on. "I dinnae believe ye have done it since ye were wee."

"I have always called ye Alex," Nala insisted. "Even if nae out loud."

The air shifted as they looked at each other. It was suddenly awkward that she sat on his lap. She wasn't sure if she should jump up or slide away slowly. She'd meant to comfort him, and it had felt natural, but now it felt different, much too intimate.

"Alex, I think…" She stopped speaking noting the heat in his eyes.

Alex pressed a soft kiss to her lips. "I am glad ye came. Feeling bad for myself does nae accomplish anything."

"We all feel that way every so often," Nala acquiesced, her voice hoarse in her own ears.

Once again, he kissed her. "Do ye wish for it?"

Nala's lips parted as her breath caught. "Do I wish for what?" Her mind was scrambled, she couldn't think about anything other than having his mouth on hers again. His hands on her. His body against hers.

"Us," Alexander replied taking her mouth with so much hunger, she let out a soft moan. It was what she wanted more than anything in her life. Him. She wanted him.

It wasn't in her nature to skirt direct questions—unless necessary—and for a second, Nala considered it. In the end, she was honest.

"I do," she replied wrapping her arms around his neck and looking straight into his eyes. "I want ye Alex. All of ye."

Their mouths collided, Alex pressed his tongue at the seam of her lips, and she parted them, gladly, so he could plunge in. Their tongue twisted and turned, in a way she'd never tire of.

Needing to feel his skin, she slid her hand under his tunic, not satisfied until touching his bare skin. Her palms traveled up his broad back and then down to his sides. The taut muscular hills and valleys were like no other man's she'd known.

Alexander's husky moan was like sinking into warm water. When he trailed his mouth from hers, down the side of her throat, and on further. Nala arched her back, her hands continuously caressing his back.

The strings that held her bodice together fell away easily when he pulled them. Scant seconds later, the cool air of the room touched her bared breasts and Nala shivered. Not from the cold, but the sensual sensation it stirred within her depths.

"Ye are perfect," Alex murmured, his face between the mounds, suckling and licking from one breast to the other. He took the tip of one into his mouth, his tongue circling it until Nala could scarcely breathe. Trails of desire streamed up and down her body and she turned to straddle him.

The feel of his evident arousal stoked the embers of desire until they took on a new life, blazing out of control.

"I need ye," Nala gasped. "Please Alex." She rubbed against him, and Alex's head lifted taking her mouth again.

Grasping her bottom, he ground against her, his breathing coming in harsh breaths. "I cannae. Ye ken I cannae."

"Please?" Nala demanded, then let out a gasp when he lowered her to the floor.

"I will help ye find relief," Alex said, then pulled his tunic off over his head before lowering to lay with her.

The feel of his skin against her breasts was as close to heaven as she felt she could go while alive. Perhaps being fully his would be the only thing better.

Then he took her mouth with his and she drank him in greedily while running her hands up and down his back, never tiring of the feel of his skin.

Alex pulled her skirts up and ran his hand up her inner thigh, his fingers caressing the sensitive skin slowly in circles marking trails of delight.

It didn't help douse her desire but had the opposite effect. Did the man know what he was doing? He said he would help her, instead as a result of his caresses, she was like a burning inferno.

Just as she was about to tell him to stop, he reached the apex between her legs, his fingers delving between her sex, sliding up and down through her moistness. Nala trembled as the heat became so intense, she thought it would consume her.

When she gasped, Alex lifted to look at her then lowered his face against hers.

"Allow me," he whispered against her ear.

"Aye," she whispered.

Somehow, he splayed her open with one hand while stroking the nub at her center. Nala bucked up into his hand, the sensations so overwhelming that she called out his name.

Alex took her mouth and began moving his finger over the perfect place. A place she never knew existed and suddenly she didn't care if the fire consumed her, Nala gave in to it.

The room spun and she lost control, clinging to him as every part of her being came to life. Stars exploded behind her lids and when she let out a cry of pleasure Alex's mouth covered hers and muffled the sound.

He continued the assault until she plummeted once again, this time not as wildly, but just as wonderfully.

Then he pressed soft kisses over her face until her breathing slowed.

Nala clung to him, her fingers digging into his back as she reveled in the wonder of what he'd done to her.

"Nala, look at me." Alex sounded worried. "Are ye mad at me?"

A burst of laughter escaped when she opened her eyes to find him looking as if he'd just done something horrible and was prepared to be punished.

Nala pressed a kiss to his parted lips. "Why would I be mad at the man who just showed me what paradise truly is?"

Relief spread across his handsome face. "Ye are truly an astonishing woman." He rolled to his back, both lying on the floor staring up at the ceiling.

When she peered down at him, his arousal remained quite obvious. "Do ye need help with that?"

He shook his head. "I think it's best we go from here before someone comes looking for ye."

Alex stood and pulled her up, then he expertly tied the stays of the blouse before giving her an appraising look. "Perhaps ye should do something with yer hair."

"Ye will nae act differently when around me, will ye?" Nala asked in what she hoped was a casual tone. In actuality, her heart continued to flutter in her chest, and she had to fight to not throw herself into his arms and demand he kiss her again.

At the same time, if Alexander began looking at her differently, it would be obvious that they'd shared a very private moment. Nala blew out a breath, could she keep an expression of indifference when around him?

"Differently?" He looked puzzled.

"Aye," Nala said as she raked her fingers through her hair and began to twist the strands into a neat braid. "Ye ken those heated looks men give women they desire. Behave like before, ignore me for the most part."

He shook his head. "I didnae ignore ye."

She waved away his comment. "I think ye do." Suddenly her breath caught. "Oh, goodness, I just remembered. My parents are here."

Running out of the room and down the corridor as fast as she could, Nala dashed into the kitchens and grabbed a tray from a befuddled maid. "I will take this." She hesitated. "Where exactly were ye taking it?"

Walking into the great room, all she could think of was that everyone would notice her and see something different about her. There had to be something different as she'd never, ever been so overcome with passion.

Alexander had to be the most magical man who'd ever existed.

CHAPTER TEN

G RANT LANDS WERE lush with hills covered in deep green grasses. Plump bushes and bright purple flowers carpeted the ground along the edges of the road they traveled on. The dirt path winded past trees that stretched overhead casting shadows on travelers.

Alexander and his entourage of ten warriors, including his brother Cynden, had left the keep hours earlier and would be arriving at the Grants' keep within moments.

The ride had given Alexander time to think about what his father had said about the elusive laird. Clan Ross and Clan Grant were neither allies nor foes. Instead, the two clans had ignored each other for decades. As if by some unspoken agreement, the stretches of acreage along where their lands bordered were uninhabited on both sides. Almost as if maintaining a safe distance.

From what Alexander could remember, there had been a rift between his father and the Grant. The reason was unclear. During the many hours he'd spent at his father's sick bed, Alexander had broached the subject one day.

"Clan Ross has no need for that clan. Keep yer distance from them, son," his father said before abruptly changing the subject.

Perhaps the Grant would answer why there was such a

divide between the clans.

Just past a bend, the keep came into view. The imposing castle was surrounded by stone walls low enough that they could easily be scaled. Interesting. Perhaps they didn't fear intruders, or it could be that since three sides of the keep were surrounded by water, their main defense would come from archers and warriors to the front.

Clan Grant was about the same size as Clan Ross. Scouts had informed Alexander that their warrior force was about thirty men, most trained in archery.

Moments later a contingency of horsemen rode from Grant keep and lined up across the road, blocking access to the keep.

One warrior, a broad-shouldered man about Alexander's age guided his steed in front of the others. The man had thick reddish hair that fell past his shoulders. The same shade of hair covered the bottom half of his face.

They waited in silence until Alexander and his men neared.

"I am the Ross," Alexander called out and then motioned to Cynden. "My brother Cynden. I come here to pay a visit to the Grant. I come in peace."

The man's bright blue gaze took him in, then shifted to the men with him. "I am Connor Grant, the laird's eldest son. Ye and yers have nae visited before."

"There have been changes in current events and I wish to discuss things with yer father," Alexander replied.

After a moment, the man turned his horse around and motioned for them to follow. The Grant men parted and allowed them through, then followed behind. As they rode forward, Connor gave Alexander a curious look. "That ye are laird must mean that yer da is now dead."

It wasn't a question, but Alexander felt obliged to reply, nonetheless. "Aye. Two years hence,"

The man was silent for a moment. "Be with care crossing," he warned motioning to a bridge over a water inlet across the front of the keep.

The bridge had no sides, it was flat. One misstep from the horse would send steed and rider over the sides into a bog of sorts. It was impossible to tell how deep the muddy water was.

"Is it deep?" Cynden asked Connor.

"Yer horse would sink to its neck."

Archers kept watch from atop the wall, their bows and quivers secured across their backs. Alexander had to admit, it was a good intimidation tactic.

"Interesting," Cynden said. "Yer archers can easily be shot at from those woods." He motioned to the nearest tree line.

Connor grunted. Perhaps he tried to keep from chuckling.

Upon crossing the bridge, they rode past open gates into a well-kept courtyard. Unlike Clan Ross' courtyard, this one resembled a village square. Three buildings surrounded the courtyard. On one side were stables, opposite what looked to be guard quarters, which were flanked by a large structure that was probably the family home.

They were not greeted at the front door, not that Alexander was expected. The Grant would not be caught unaware, he'd seen a man sent ahead at a gallop to inform the laird of his arrival. It was customary, in the Highlands, for one laird to greet another formally at the front entrance with a member of his family beside him.

However, it seemed the Grant did not hold to the custom.

Stable lads rushed over to take the horses after they dismounted. Connor gave them firm instructions to water and feed the animals, adding they should be with care.

Alexander ordered his men to remain outside in the courtyard, except for Cynden and Hendry, who followed him and Connor to the main house. Just inside the entry, they waited a beat to allow their eyes to become accustomed to the dim interior. Then they continued into a large room he assumed to be the great room.

The room was devoid of people, giving him the opportunity to study his surroundings. Thick embroidered tapestries hung behind the high board depicting a hunting scene. The tapestries to his left were of dogs and trees, the scene almost playful. Over the hearth was the Grant coat of arms, next to it a portrait of who he assumed was the laird and his wife. To Alexander's right, hung in a line, were two huge tapestries. The embroidered scenes of these were of people in a garden of sorts. There were horses, archers, and women seeming to be in the midst of chaos.

Just then an older man, with the same reddish hair as Connor, except sprinkled with gray, walked into the room. Behind him, two men, who were almost identical to Connor, entered.

Laird Grant was of a good stature and remained youthful in appearance. By his well-toned build, he had been a warrior all his life. When the man's steely blue eyes lifted to Alexander his lips parted, and his eyes widened as if in recognition.

"Ye are truly yer father's son. There is nae doubt," he said in a low voice. "Ye are Roderick when he was yer age." He continued to stare at Alexander then seeming to realize what he did he regained his composure. "I am Malcolm Grant, welcome to my home."

"I am Alexander Ross, this is my brother Cynden," Alexander said.

Laird Grant kept looking at him as if unable to see no one other than his father. He cleared his throat. "Ye have met my eldest son, Conner." He waved a hand to the two who'd followed him in. "My second-born sons, Broden and Gawyn."

The twins' remained stoic, neither friendly nor threatening. The only indication of a greeting was a nod from the one called Broden.

"Let us sit and speak." Laird Grant motioned to a table that was surrounded by intricately carved chairs. Alexander surmised it was the table set aside for the laird and visitors.

Three women appeared at the doorway carrying trays with meats and cheeses, breads and oils, as well as fruits. Tankards were filled and placed before them, then wooden plates were slid in front of each man so they could partake of the offerings.

"Is it just ye and yer sons?" Cynden asked. His brother was the most curious man and never shied away from asking questions. Times like these, Alexander was glad for it.

"Nae, my wife and daughter, Edina, live here as well. They have gone to visit family and will nae return until the morrow," Laird Grant clarified.

They spoke of the surrounding lands and about the village closer to the Grant keep. The entire time, Alexander felt as if he was kin to the man. For some reason, he didn't feel as if he spoke with a stranger, but someone akin to an uncle.

"Why do our clans remain so distant?" Alexander had to

ask.

LAIRD GRANT'S SONS looked to the older man as if they too wished to know the reply. The man let out a long sigh. Then he drank from his tankard. Alexander began to think he would not respond to the question, but then the man leaned forward, placing an elbow on the table.

"Yer father and I were great friends as lads. We did everything together. Trained at sword fighting. Hunted. He and I even joined the Ross guard at the same time. In that time, Clan Grant had yet to establish here on Skye."

He let out a long sigh. "My grandfather owned this place." He lifted a hand to motion at the ceiling. "But it was nae until I was twenty that Clan Grant began to grow. Upon my grandfather's death, my father was established as laird. Yer father and I had another thing in common, we both became first sons who would one day inherit the title."

He paused and shook his head sadly. "The MacLeods attacked Clan Ross. Yer grandfather asked my father to send help. My father felt he could nae. Our force was small, barely five and ten men. We needed them to defend our home. Yer grandfather was vexed and asked that I leave the Ross guard."

Everyone was silent as they pondered the information. Alexander broke the quiet with another question. "What about yer friendship with my father?"

"Understandably, yer grandfather felt as if the alliance was one-sided. He declared we could no longer be allies."

Gawyn studied Alexander and then turned to his father. "This is what ended yer friendship with Laird Ross?"

"We could no longer travel freely to one another's lands.

After a while, we rarely saw each other and lost touch."

There was something the man was not saying, Alexander felt it to his bones, but he would bide his time and wait for the right moment.

When the meal was finished, the Grant brothers invited Cynden to a tour of the training field.

"Ye must try this whiskey," Malcolm Grant said standing to pour Alexander and himself some of the amber liquid. After lifting the glasses to each other, they drank. Alexander was impressed with the smoothness of the whiskey that glided down his throat.

"It is quite good," he admitted. "Is it made here?"

The Grant's face split with a grin. "Aye, it is, I will send a few bottles with ye. I have tried many others, but none can compare to the one my friend Angus Brown makes."

The man studied him. "I cannae stop looking at ye without thinking of Roderick. How long has it been since his death?"

"Just over two years," Alexander replied.

The man lowered his head. "I wish to have seen him before…" He let out a breath. "Forgive me. I keep reverting to the past. There must be a reason for yer visit."

"In the past years, there has not been peace for Clan Ross. For years, we battled against the Mackinnons until defeating them just a pair of seasons past. In the last months, we were attacked by Clan MacLeod, who came by sea. They were soon defeated and returned from where they came. As of late, there have been random attacks on defenseless people. The men were caught, and I had them executed." Alexander met the older man's gaze. "I am tired and came to speak to ye and ensure that my clan continues to live in peace. Assure myself that there will nae be any threat from yer clan."

Malcolm frowned. "Ye have faced much for being so young. I knew of yer clashes with Clan Mackinnon and also of ye finally defeating that dolt of a laird. He didnae deserve to be laird."

Servants shuffled in to remove the remains of the food. A young lass neared and stood waiting to be acknowledged. Laird Grant turned to her. "Yes, lass."

"Laird, Cook would like to ken if yer guests will remain for last meal."

It was interesting that the young woman didn't seem intimidated by the laird, but at ease asking the question. In Alexander's opinion, it spoke well of the man's treatment of his servants.

Before he could reply Alexander interjected, "We cannae remain much longer. There is much to be done at Keep Ross."

"There ye have the answer," Malcolm stated. "Tell Cook to prepare sacks with sustenance for Laird Ross and his accompaniment to eat on the way back. Also, four bottles of whiskey."

The servant went away, once again leaving them in the large silent room.

The laird waited for Alexander to continue speaking. He'd hoped for a reply to his question, but since it didn't come, he'd have to ask in a different way. Make it clear.

"Were ye nae bothered by the MacLeods?"

Laird Grant shook his head. "This keep is in a very good location. Birlinns would have to travel into the narrow inlet of water to reach us by sea. By foot, they would be quickly spotted. Because of where this keep is, we have rarely seen any kind of attempts to breach our home. In the past, there have been attacks on the village, unsuccessful attempts to take it over."

"Were ye aware of the attacks on my clan by the MacLeods?"

The Grant shook his head. "Not until it was over. A traveling peddler came with the news of what had occurred." After hesitating for a moment, he asked, "Did ye lose many men?"

"A few, aye. My brother, Gavin, was gravely injured, but thankfully recovered."

"Did ye ever build a wall facing out to sea?" the man asked.

"Nae. I have men posted on three sides, they can see in every direction. The attacks came not just by sea, but from land as well. We were able to keep them from entering the keep."

The Grant seemed pensive. "Yer father was quite good at keeping attacks at bay. I admired that about him."

The opening allowed Alexander to once again approach the subject of the rift between the Grant and his father. "Aye, he was. Ye seem to have fond memories of my father. The few times he spoke about ye, he didnae seem to hold ye in bad regard as well. Why did ye and he never speak again?"

When the man's lips curved, it was obvious he realized he had provided an opportunity for Alexander to broach the subject again. "I will tell ye with the promise that ye will nae tell anyone else."

The reason for the rift became more interesting and Alexander nodded. "I will nae share what ye say."

"Very well." The man looked across the room to the large portrait over the hearth. "My wife, Una, and yer father were in love and planned to marry. She was Clan Mackinnon."

Alexander fought not to gawk openly at the man. Was that part of the reason for their long battle between his clan and the Mackinnons?

Laird Grant continued, "Her father approached mine and arranged a marriage between her and I." He shook his head. "I could nae disobey my father, and she could nae disobey hers. Roderick went for her in an attempt to take her and run away together. When she refused it broke his heart."

Silence stretched as Alexander absorbed the information. Why had his father not told him? It would have made it easier for him to approach the Grant to suggest an alliance. Did he not wish for it? Why had he held the grudge for so many years? His parents had never seemed to be overly loving, but they'd seemed content in the marriage.

That the Grant's wife was a Mackinnon meant that Clan Grant could have been allied to the man his clan battled for many years.

"Were ye and the Mackinnon allies?" Alexander asked.

"We were nae foe or ally. I suppose ye can say, we have kept ourselves separate from the other clans on this isle for many years."

Alexander wasn't sure if it was a mark of cowardice or intelligence that Clan Grant kept their distance from strife. "When the attackers were caught, they headed to yer lands. Had they approached ye for harbor?"

"I was nae aware of any attacks. Few people, other than those visiting families or peddlers, come from the east."

The reply didn't sound firmly in the negative; however, there was nothing Alexander could say to challenge his host.

He allowed his gaze back to the portrait. The woman pictured next to Roderick was indeed a beauty. At the same time, his mother was also an attractive woman, even at her current age of fifty.

"How old were ye and father when ye married?"

The Grant seemed perplexed by the question. "We had both just turned nine and ten. Very young still. Una was six and ten. Yer father married yer mother within months."

Alexander's mind whirled with so many more questions. Like was his mother aware of his father being in love with someone else?

"Did my mother ken?"

"I dinnae ken. I doubt it." Laird Grant looked at Alexander. "Yer father and I saw each other again when we were both about five and twenty, during a competition. I wish now that I would have embraced him and made more of an effort to…" The man stopped speaking and shook his head. "I suppose what is done is done."

They had all been so young, Alexander mused. "It is a sad thing that ye and my father lost yer friendship."

Roderick Grant's face brightened. "I hope that ye and Conner get to know each other better. He will be laird one day and ye would be a good mentor to him. Alexander, our clans can be open to each other. My lands to the east join yers. Perhaps we can meet for a friendly tournament, to allow our people to ken each other."

"Not allies, but on good terms then?" Alexander wasn't ready to propose an alliance.

The man opposite him nodded. "Friends."

Alexander liked the idea. "I agree. I would like to extend an invitation that ye and yers come to Keep Ross. Our clans have remained apart too long."

His companion looked down to the table, seeming to suddenly be overcome by emotion. The Grant blew out a breath, blinking rapidly before lifting his gaze. "Thank ye, Alexander for coming. I am so very glad ye did."

The man's eyes became shiny, and he hastily wiped at them with his tunic sleeve. "Forgive an old man for his lack of control."

Alexander chuckled. "It is our secret."

When the Grant studied him, Alexander met his eyes. The man reached out and placed a hand on his shoulder. "It is apparent, ye are a good laird. Yer father would be so very proud."

ONCE IN THE courtyard, Alexander again reiterated the invitation to the Grant for a visit before he and his entourage mounted.

Satchels of food were brought to them as well as the promised bottles of whiskey. Laird Grant waved them away, a warm expression on his face. It felt almost as if he'd visited an uncle or other close male relative and Alexander couldn't help feeling sad that his father and the man had allowed such a close relationship to fade.

"I enjoyed getting to ken the Grant brothers. They remind me of us. Bantering and bickering, whilst it is obvious they care for each other. Once we spent time together, the twins were quite funny," Cynden said. "I wish Knox would have come."

"Someone had to remain to be there for the people," Alexander replied. "I too enjoyed my visit with the laird. He seems to be a kind man."

"It is a shame he and Father lost touch. Why would they? It seemed as if the Grant held fond memories," Cynden asked making Alexander wish he could share with his brother.

Finally he replied, "Aye, he did. The cause of the rift is nae my story to tell. I will say, they were both too proud to bridge the gap and it is a shame."

The ride back to the keep was a pleasant one. They stopped only once to water the horses and allow them to rest before continuing. It gave Alexander time to think about what the Grant had said to him. It made sense that the attackers would feel at home hiding on Grant lands as the laird's wife was a Mackinnon. If the laird was indeed unaware of what occurred, then they could roam back and forth freely. Finally, he knew why the attackers had eluded being caught for so long. They'd been hiding on Grant lands.

They arrived at the keep in time for last meal, although they were not very hungry as the Grant's cook had prepared bountiful and delicious packs of cheese, bread, dried meat, and even sweet tarts for their travel.

Once in the courtyard, the warriors went with the horses to brush down the steeds and release them either to the corrals or into stalls in the stables. Alexander and Cynden went into the house greeted by the sight of an orderly and almost empty great room.

His eyes went straight to the portrait of his father and mother. She sat in a chair, his father standing beside it, his hand possessively on her shoulder. Both had stoic expressions, and he couldn't help but wonder how they'd felt for one another during that time.

CHAPTER ELEVEN

"Nala?" Sencha's voice brought Nala out of her daydreaming. Once again, she'd been reliving being in Alexander's arms. As hard as she tried to distract herself from thinking of him, the interlude with him was constantly in her mind.

"Sorry. I was considering what to do next," Nala lied as she plucked a flower to add to the basket she carried.

Sencha giggled. "Ye are quite distracted. Ye just plucked a milkweed…again." Her friend pointed at her basket.

There were more weeds than flowers strewn haphazardly in the basket and Nala gaped at her rather unappealing harvest. "They are useful to make tonics."

They'd been walking not too far from the keep, enjoying the sunny afternoon and each other's company. It was Sencha's first visit since Nala had arrived. Perfect timing as she found herself in need of a diversion from Alexander and the useless husband hunt.

Nala smiled at her friend. "I am so glad ye are here. I have missed our visits."

"We only just returned from my grandmother's funeral. It was a pitiful affair. Only three mourners came. Father says it is because all of grandmother's acquaintances have already died."

Nala shook her head. "That is sad. I was nae aware ye went

to the Isle of Mull."

They stopped under a shade tree and Nala spread a thin blanket for them to sit on. Then she dug out two apples for them to eat. "How long were ye gone?"

"A sennight," Sencha replied. "It seemed like longer. It is a lonely desolate place where my aunt and uncle live. They remained mostly because of the family land. My aunt admits to being tired of having to travel so far to reach the village."

The breeze blew across her face and Nala closed her eyes. At once, the picture of Alexander over her, watching intently as she came undone formed, and she opened her eyes.

"Tell me my friend, what has yer head in the clouds," Sencha demanded. "And do nay say nothing. I will ken if ye lie."

To her horror, her face heated and she was sure every inch of it was bright red. Even if Nala tried to hide, Sencha could easily see how affected she was.

"Ye must swear on yer life that ye will nae tell a living soul," Nala said, her mind tumbling over what to disclose.

Sencha's wide grin was akin to a satisfied cat. "I can tell it has to do with a man. Who did ye kiss?"

Shocked at how obvious she was, Nala's mouth fell open. "What do ye mean?"

"What else would have ye so distracted, barely able to keep yer mind still enough to hear one sentence I say?" Sencha said in a sing-song tone. "Ye are in love."

"Love?" Nala rolled her eyes. "I am nae in love."

Her friend gave her a pointed look, waiting for Nala to continue.

"Very well. I did kiss someone… more than just once. A long kiss… it was like nothing else I've ever experienced."

Sencha's mouth formed a perfect circle, and her eyebrows lifted so high, they disappeared under the waves that framed her face. "Who did ye kiss?" she asked slowly. "Go on tell me."

Although there was no one about who could overhear, Nala still turned to both sides just to be sure. "Alexander."

"What?" Sencha screeched. "Nae…" Her tone tuned almost reverent. "Ye kissed the laird?"

"Shhhh," Nala hissed. "Keep yer voice down. That is why I cannae tell ye any secrets, ye are so very loud."

Sencha lifted a hand to her brow and fell backwards, pretending to swoon and then abruptly sat up. "Tell me everything."

"There is nae much to tell. The first time, I was walking along the shoreline. I am nae sure why he kissed me. It was short… sweet. This last time it was in what looked to be a healer's depository. It was passionate, and we embraced…" She stopped, not wishing to disclose what had followed. "I found him looking out a window…in the healer's shop. He seemed so despondent."

"And ye did yer duty to the laird by lifting his spirits?" Sencha fell into a fit of laughter. "Oh my."

"Stop it," Nala said, unable to keep a straight face. "I hugged him. He is a childhood friend after all. Then we kissed. It was the most natural of things. I am sure it will nae happen again."

Sencha sobered. "Why?"

"When he marries, it will have to be a match that will bring progress to the clan. He is the laird and cannae marry just anyone."

"Do ye wish him to marry ye?"

At the question, her chest tightened.

Did she?

Was she in love with Alexander or besotted because of what had occurred between them? If Nala was to be honest with herself, the thought of sharing such an intimate moment with someone other than him was unpalatable. No, she could not picture being with another man.

"It matters not how I feel or what I wish for, so I do nay think about it, much less allow myself wish for it," Nala answered honestly.

"That is a smart thing to do," Sencha remarked, her gaze moving toward the keep. "What will ye do when someone is chosen for ye to marry?"

Nala shrugged. "I will refuse. They cannae force me to marry against my will. I would run away before marrying someone not of my choosing."

Was there anywhere she could go? Nala considered that her relatives in England would turn her around and send her right back to Skye. Her father's sister had already hosted her for most of her life and had given up on finding Nala a suitable match. There was no option to go to her mother's family. It was much too far to travel. Besides, her mother had lost touch with her remaining relatives after her parents died.

"I will have to figure out where exactly to go," Nala said. "Where can I go?"

Sencha shrugged. "I doubt yer parents would force ye. Ye may end up marrying out of guilt when yer mother reminds ye over and again that it is yer fault she has no grandchildren."

"My brother can father children. I am sure he will marry." Nala frowned. "He has been gone too long. He should return soon." Her brother, Belhar, was an importer to mainland Scotland. He and Sencha's brother, whom he traveled with, were rarely on Skye as they spent most of their time on ships between the West Indies and Scotland.

"Yer brother, like mine, are never still long enough to marry, much less produce heirs," Sencha said with a huff. "They are wasting the best years of their lives."

"Indeed they are," Nala agreed. "Although I am glad for his absence as he would nae hesitate to find a husband, not just for me, but ye as well."

"Ye should marry my brother, and I can marry yers. Then we will nae have anything more to worry about."

Both made a face at the thought and dissolved into fits of laughter.

"Look," Sencha pointed toward the road that led to the keep. "Visitors come."

They watched as an entourage consisting of a coach and ten warriors moved at a leisurely pace. Within moments they were met by Ross warriors. There was an exchange and then the visitors were escorted toward the keep.

"I wonder who that is?" Sencha asked, her gaze locked to the traveling party.

"Clan Grant," Nala replied. "I recognize the coat of arms on the banner."

Interesting that neither Ainslie nor Lady Ross had mentioned anything about visitors. Then again, Nala had been distracted for the last pair of days by Sencha's visit. Still, they'd spent time together in the sitting room and at meals.

Perhaps it was an unexpected visit.

"Should we go and see what occurs?" Sencha stood to

watch. "I am very curious."

Nala rose to stand beside her friend. "I have always thought Clan Ross and Clan Grant are nae on friendly terms. Neither are they enemies, I suppose," she added.

The flowers in Nala's basket had quickly wilted. However, the hardier weeds looked as if they'd never been plucked from the ground.

Nala dumped the contents of her basket. "I promised Lady Ross we'd pick flowers for the tables," Nala reminded Sencha. "Let us pick a few wildflowers and then we have the excuse of placing flowers on the tables and we can eavesdrop on whatever conversation occurs."

BY THE TIME Nala and Sencha arrived at the keep, the visitors had been taken from the great room. She'd gathered from one of the maids, that the laird's brothers and the Grant's sons had gone to the practice field. And the Grant's wife and daughter to the parlor with Lady Ross and Ainslie.

It would be impolite for Nala and Sencha to enter now, besides, she needed to change as the dress she wore had grass stains.

They took their time arranging the flowers in vases and set them about the room. Afterwards, Nala suggested they return back outdoors to watch the men practice at swordplay or archery. They went out a side door and sat on one of the benches along the wall. A canopy of ivy-laden trellises provided them with shade from the sunny day. Ross warriors stood around watching two men battle.

It was Cynden and a red-haired man, who sparred, circling, thrusting their swords, evading strikes. By the smooth movements of each man, they were both well-practiced in the art of swordplay. And by the intensity in which they sparred, both were competitive. By the time, they were told to stop, both were drenched in sweat, chests heaving.

Next, Alexander paired with another man who looked to be almost identical to the one Cynden had been fighting.

"Do ye think they are twins?" Sencha asked in a low tone, as if she didn't want to disturb the combatants. "The three men look to be brothers, but two are much more alike in features and stature."

"I wondered the same," Nala replied, her eyes glued to Alexander, who effectively blocked a downward strike. "How can they keep from injuring one another?"

"By weighing yer opponent's skill level and adjusting accordingly," a deep voice stated causing both Nala and Sencha to jerk toward the doorway they'd come through.

Knox walked closer, his gaze moving from them to the sword fight. "Alex is a much better fighter, but he holds back so as not to insult the visitor."

The archer leaned on the wall next to their bench, seeming not to have any plans to go to the practice field.

Sencha slid a look up his long lean body until reaching Knox's face. "Are ye going to join them? Would ye compete with a sword or bow?"

After a moment, Knox shrugged. "I will do what Alex deems for me. I prefer nae to do anything at all." It was then Nala noted the sweat on his brow and the pallor of his skin.

She stood and touched the back of her hand to his face. "Ye are sick and feverish. Should be abed. Go on then, I will send someone with cool cloths and tonic."

"I'd forgotten how stubborn ye are," Knox said, but he didn't argue. "I should be out there representing my family and clan." He shook his head as if trying to regain focus.

Sencha narrowed her eyes up at him. "Unless ye wish for the visiting laird to think yer family to be mad and delusional, it is best ye dinnae show yerself."

Nala couldn't help the bark of laughter that escaped. Unfortunately, it came out a bit loud and the group of men turned to look in their direction. After a moment, the men returned to their conversations, seeming to disregard their presence.

"Come Knox," Nala insisted, motioning to the doorway. As they entered the house, she turned one last time to glance toward the practice field. Alexander watched them.

After seeing Knox to his bed and asking maids to bring cool water, she placed a wet cloth on his brow and ordered for an herb called feverfew to be boiled to make a tonic.

She remained with Knox until he fell asleep, and his face was cooler to the touch.

FEELING SATISFIED THAT Knox would be well, Nala went to her room and washed up so that she could wear a clean dress as it was almost time for last meal.

Sencha sat up on the bed, she'd been napping and woke with a start. "Ye should nae have let me sleep so long," she complained and then her features softened. "How fares Knox?"

"His fever has broken, and he sleeps. I am sure after some rest he will be well."

"I am glad to hear it." Sencha reached up to brush errant

strands from her face. "I must do something about my hair and dress and decide what I should say in greeting when I see Alexander." She gave Nala an impish grin.

"Ye will say nothing other than what courtesy dictates," Nala replied giving her friend a steely stare.

It was not long after that they finally descended the stairs and walked into the great room. Lady Ross and the visiting women were already at the table where they took their meals. When Nala and Sencha neared, Lady Ross motioned for them to sit.

"These lovely ladies are daughters of my dear friends. This is Nala Maclaren and Sencha Anderson." Lady Ross smiled at her. "Ye look lovely."

A woman who Nala presumed to be Lady Grant smiled warmly. "I am called Una, and this is my daughter Leah." She looked to her daughter with pride. "Leah recently returned from studies in Inverness."

Leah scanned both Nala and Sencha, seeming to find them lacking by the downturn of her lips.

"Nala and her brother grew up with my sons. She was especially close to Cynden," Lady Ross explained.

At the statement, Leah took interest in Nala, her blue eyes taking her in. "Ye are nae married?"

Lady Ross chuckled. "Our Nala is an independent sort. She also recently returned from years of living in London. We hope to help in the quest for a suitable husband."

Although it proved quite difficult, Nala managed what she hoped was a pleasant expression. She didn't want Leah to know anything about her. Something about the woman put her on alert. "And ye Leah, are ye married or betrothed?"

Just as the younger woman opened her mouth to reply, her gaze shifted to the entrance. Laird Grant walked next to Alexander, the two lairds presenting an attractive picture.

Although the Grant was older, he remained a handsome man. His thick reddish hair was sprinkled with gray at the temples framing a handsome face. He wore a sash across one broad shoulder that was tied off at his trim waist. The tartan colors were flattering to his fair skin. Although he was a bit shorter than Alexander, he was still a tall man.

Nala took the opportunity to study Alexander, who looked wickedly handsome in a bright white tunic, over which the green and black tartan was draped and pinned to his shoulder. His ebony tresses were brushed back from his face, bringing attention to his exquisite features. Seeming to sense her regard, his gaze met hers just for a beat. It was as if he touched her by the way her body instantly reacted. When he looked back to the laird, the corners of his lips lifted just a bit. It was barely perceptible, but Nala saw it. Then he looked back to the table and his right brow lifted.

Nala almost gasped. He was purposely ignoring her request for him to act normally. She looked around to the others, hoping they'd not noticed. When she dared to slide a glance to Sencha, her friend mimicked Alexander's brow lift.

Behind Alexander and the Grant entered Cynden, who was in deep conversation with the broader of the brothers. The other two brothers brought up the rear.

"Ye must remind me of yer son's names," Lady Ross commented.

Lady Grant smiled. The woman, unlike her daughter, had a warm presence. "The eldest, who walks with Cynden is called

Connor. The twins are Gawyn and Broden. The best way to tell them apart is that Gawyn has a scar that breaks through his right brow. Otherwise, they are almost identical."

Nala and Sencha studied the twins. It was most interesting that two humans could look that much alike. Unlike their sister, who had bright red hair and pale skin, the twins' hair was a dark auburn and they had olive skin like their mother. The eldest, Connor, was of the same coloring as Leah and their father.

The meal was served, and Lady Ross kept the discussion on safe topics of gardening, the weather, and descriptions of the local village.

Lady Grant did the same, regaling them with the different wares available at a market that had been started by locals near Grant lands. It had somehow grown so large that many merchants traveled to sell their wares there.

Sencha was practically salivating. "I have heard that there are fabrics sold there that are so silky, they slip through the fingers."

Lady Grant nodded. "I must admit, there are so many things to see and touch, I have yet to sample everything. Ye must all come visit and we will plan an outing."

"Mother will be most delighted," Sencha exuded, bright pink blossoming on her cheeks.

There were murmurs as Alexander stood and held up a cup. He welcomed the Grants formally and toasted to the laird's health.

The Grant then stood and thanked Alexander, he too toasting to the Ross' good health. The man grinned widely. "Perhaps by the end of the visit, we can come up with a way for our clans to once again be united." The man looked to where his wife and Leah sat.

Leah beamed.

Nala's stomach plummeted.

CHAPTER TWELVE

THE VISIT WAS going well, although if Alexander were to be honest, he was restless. A part of him wanted to mount and ride without a destination in mind. He yearned for time alone, to go away from the responsibilities and the conflicting emotions that had him unsettled. Was it that he'd grown so accustomed to chaos that peace unsettled him?

As last meal was concluding, the Grant was discussing the hunting on his lands with Cynden, who'd asked about it. Thankfully, his brother seemed to understand Alexander and without a word had known the announcement the Grant had made did not sit well with him.

An alliance with Clan Grant would be beneficial since their lands expanded almost the entire northwestern coast of the isle.

A union, however, was another story.

He'd noted the expressions at the women's table at the Grant stating he desired a union. His daughter, a pretty lass, had come to life, her eager expression almost frightening. His mother, on the other hand, was not as enthusiastic. She'd given him a questioning look. Then there was Nala, who with eyebrows lifted, looked from him to Leah Grant, studying the other woman. Finally, she'd met his gaze for a split second, and he thought he had seen a flash of something. Perhaps hurt?

Of course he'd not marry Leah Grant. He'd have to ensure the Grant understood that it wasn't an option.

IT WAS LATE by the time the Grant had finally retired. Admittedly, he and his brother had enjoyed hearing tales of their father's youth. A time before their mother had entered his life and before the lairds had ended their friendship.

Alone in the great room, Alexander considered going to find his bed, but he was restless and instead went outside. He walked to the wall and climbed up to stand at a corner of it, so that he could see across toward the village and to his right, the expanse of the sea. It was dark, but the sounds of the waves were enough to soothe him. A light wind brought the salty air. Like a lover's caress, the wind blew across his skin and tussled his hair, blowing it across his face.

His duties were many, but he didn't mind it. It was his legacy after all. And yet there were days when he wondered what it would be like to be a villager, a baker or a cobbler, whose only responsibility was to make bread, or shoes. The only people that counted on those men were their wives and bairns. Unlike him who carried the weight of not only his family, but the entire clan.

"Alex," Cynden said. "Is something wrong?"

He turned to see his brother's sleepy face and almost laughed. In that moment, Cynden looked to be about two and twelve. Especially when he yawned and rubbed his eyes.

"I was too restless to sleep. Thought some time here would settle my mind," Alexander replied. "Why are ye up? Go back to bed."

"Ainslie opened the shutters to get fresh air and saw ye. She said ye may be considering jumping and ending it all." Cynden chuckled. "She joked, but then I could nae go back to sleep."

Alexander peered down to the jagged hillside that sloped from the wall toward the sandy shore. "I would nae die if I jumped. It is possible I suppose that after I rolled down the hill I could be trampled by a startled sheep."

"Ye could hit yer head and bleed to death," Cynden said peering over the edge like Alexander had. "It would be quite a fall. I think ye would at least break an arm or leg."

They stood side by side looking out to the sea. "Strange that the Grant has such high regard for Father and yet never tried to bridge the gap between them."

"I believe he tried," Alexander replied. "Da was quite stubborn."

Without speaking, they walked to the steps and descended, making their way back into the house and up the stairs to their respective bedchambers.

His mind remained on the visit and on the day ahead. He'd have to leave Cynden to any lairdship duties, so that he could entertain the visiting laird. He removed all his clothes and stood bare in front of the washstand next to the hearth. Dipping a cloth into the cool water, he washed his body and then dried it.

As he slipped between the blankets without bothering with a nightshirt, his mind conjured the picture of Nala coming undone by him, his fingers bringing her to climax. She'd been so utterly beautiful in that moment. His sex came to life, hardening, jutting from his body in expectation. Alexander wrapped his hand around the thick shaft, sliding it up and down, his hips reacting by thrusting into the motions. Soon his breathing became jagged and his movements faster, the hand tighter, heat pooled at the base of his sex. Alexander arched, the back of his head sinking into the bedding as he stroked. When his body shuddered in release, he let out a harsh moan and then went slack. Already his eyes were heavy as sleep claimed him.

First meal was sparse. Outside a steady rain fell, which meant there would not be many people seeking a hearing. Unfortunately, it also meant they'd be confined indoors until it let up.

Dressed in a simple tunic, breeches, and boots, Alexander ate his meal. The Grant had sent a message with his wife that he was indisposed and would join him for midday meal. The man had imbibed a bit more than usual, his wife had disclosed in a conspiratorial whisper.

Alexander met with the council to discuss the latest issues. Mostly they had to decide on preparations for winter and choosing which farmers would supply the keep with necessary supplies for the following seasons. It was something that had fallen by the wayside lately, but a tradition that would bring much-needed normalcy as farmers would compete by showcasing the best of their harvest.

The village would celebrate with a fete and there would be music and friendly competitions between the keep guards and the villagers. It had been several years since they'd been able to have such events, as the ongoing battles had kept the clan's people in fear.

When Alexander ended the meeting, Nala's father went to find his daughter to visit and see about her. The Grant was in the great room, breaking his fast with a plain meal of broth and bread. Red-rimmed eyes met his and he motioned for Alexander to join him.

"I must apologize for my late rising," the man stated.

Alexander gave him an amused look. "It is understandable."

"Whilst I bragged about my whiskey, ye didnae tell me about the Clan Ross flavorful ales." The Grant studied the empty room, his eyes coming to rest over the hearth. "Not much has changed, except for that portrait."

"What would ye like to do today?" Alexander changed the subject. As much as he enjoyed hearing about his father the night before, he didn't want to linger in the past. "I had planned a trip to the village, if the weather warms."

The Grant waved Alexander's words away. "I dinnae wish to be a bother. Instead, we should discuss ways in which our clans can help one another."

"Some of the council remains. We can do that," Alexander stated, hoping to avoid speaking of the Grant's daughter.

The Grant grinned as if delighted. "Grand idea."

Moments later, the Clan Ross council sat with the Grant and his eldest son in the parlor to discuss. Knox, Cynden, and Nala's father were present, as well as the village constable.

Nala's father and the Grant were soon engrossed in discussions of the rules between the clans, the fact that his lands bordered Clan Grant's meant the man had a personal interest in the subject.

As the conversation continued, Alexander excused himself,

stating he would return shortly.

Nala sat in front of the hearth, her gaze on the fire. When he approached, she started and peered up at him. There was something akin to annoyance in the beautiful brown depths.

"Should ye nae be in there?" She motioned toward the parlor. "My father was pulled away before I could ask about my horse."

Alexander lowered to the chair next to hers. "I will return, I needed to walk out and clear my head for a moment." He looked around the empty room. "Where are the other women? Yer friend?"

"Everyone left to give me privacy to visit with my father," Nala said with a shrug and then pinned him with a narrowed look. "What ye really wish to ken is where Leah is."

It took a moment for him to remember the name. His lips curved at the fact that it obviously bothered Nala. "I can seek her out later."

He was enjoying goading her. "Or ye can speak to her."

Nala looked down, then sharply back up at him. "Why tell me? She's barely acknowledged my presence. If it is a message ye wish to relay to her, tell it to someone else." She returned her attention to the fire.

"Are ye jealous?" Alexander couldn't help trying to get a reaction out of the beauty.

Nala's gaze snapped to him. "Of course not. Ye are free to seek who ye want."

"I am aware of it. In this circumstance, I believe her father wishes for clan unity based on marriage."

When she looked at him, Alexander pretended not to notice. "I suppose it is nae a terrible thing."

"I dinnae wish to have this conversation with ye. Ye should talk to yer brother about it." There was a slight quiver to her bottom lip, it was just enough to get his attention and consider that perhaps he'd pushed her too far.

He leaned forward. "I prefer talking to ye. Yer company settles me." It wasn't a lie, she did something to him, calming him inwardly. While physically, he had to fight to keep from touching her. "Do ye nae like me?"

Nala looked up at the ceiling. "Of course I like ye. We have known each other practically since birth. My birth anyway, as ye are what five or six years older than I. However, I prefer nae to speak of yer romantic conquests. A man should only speak to another man about such things."

"What if I want to speak about what happened between us? How watching ye come undone is forefront in my mind constantly. I find it hard to nae touch ye. To have ye in my arms again."

Her cheek pinkened, but she refused to meet his gaze. "Ye should nae speak to anyone about that." Then she added, "Ye will nae, will ye?"

Alexander would not goad her about it. "Nae. I will only think about it and share my thoughts with ye."

With a fiery annoyed expression, Nala jumped to her feet. "Why bring it up after admitting ye like the idea of marrying another?"

He couldn't help but smile, loving the sight of the angry woman. Her plump lips parted as she caught her breath. Her narrowed eyes taking him in, she stood with both hands balled into fists. She was a beautiful sight.

Alexander shook his head in a futile attempt to dislodge

the thought of throwing her over his shoulder and taking her to his bed. To hell with the repercussions.

Before he could say any more, Nala turned on her heel and rushed from the room.

He was about to go after her when the other women entered the room. His mother seemed to have become fast friends with Grant's wife as they strolled into the room arm in arm, chatting amicably. Behind them were Ainslie, who gave him a bored look, and Leah.

At seeing him Leah's face brightened, and she came directly to him. Looking up to him, she smiled coyly. "It seems the rain has finally let up. I would enjoy a stroll about the courtyard. Father says it is one of the best ones on Skye."

"I am due back in the parlor…" Alexander began just as he spotted her father and the other men entering the room.

Leah followed his line of sight. "Good timing on my part as it seems the meeting is over."

There was little he could do. The lass was attractive, if one preferred redheads, which he didn't particularly. Alexander supposed a man could never judge a woman based on hair color. It seemed she had an agreeable disposition.

He offered his arm, and she slipped her hand into the crook of it, her touch delicate. They made their way outside, but not before he caught an amused look from Cynden.

The rain had abated, but the sky remained gloomy and the ground muddy. "Are ye sure to wish to walk about? Yer skirts will get muddy."

Leah released his arm, pulled the hem of her skirt on one side, and tucked it into her waistband bringing the hem to just above her ankles. "There we are, no mucky skirts."

She wore sturdy boots, making him think she'd planned to go for an outdoor trek. Alexander motioned toward the side of the keep and they walked toward the side that would give them a view of the lands leading toward the village.

Despite himself, Alexander enjoyed Leah's company. She asked questions about his life there and about the village. She seemed particularly interested in the seashore, comparing it to where she lived explaining the shorelines of the inlet were much calmer.

"I find the smell of the sea soothes my soul," Leah said, her eyes closed. "Do ye nae think something about it is magical?"

Alexander considered her question. "The sea is alive, it is what beckons us."

"Ah," Leah replied smiling at him. "I suppose ye are right. It is full of life. It can give pleasure or lure a person to their death." She gave a one shoulder shrug. "How do ye feel about Father's very obvious wish for us?"

The question caught Alexander by surprise. The woman was certainly bold and did not shirk from asking direct questions.

"I wish for an alliance with yer father. As allies, we could help one other, both in peace and at war."

"That is nae what I meant," Leah persisted. "Us."—she motioned between them—"Ye and I being the reason for an unbreakable unity."

"A marriage does nae always keep the peace between clans." He thought of the reason Clan Grant and his father had parted ways. Obviously, Leah was never told. Alexander met her gaze and decided to answer as boldly as she'd asked.

"I dinnae plan to marry ye."

He'd expected some sort of outburst, perhaps tears for his lack of caring. Leah inhaled and blew out a breath. She stood stock-still for a few moments, lips pressed into a thin line. "I could say ye made unwanted advances. Ye would have to marry me to keep from angering father."

Her gaze remained straight ahead, not reacting when he took a step away. "Would ye do that?"

Leah flashed a smile at him, it didn't reach her eyes. "Of course not. I dinnae wish to be married to someone who does nae value me." She threaded her arm through his. "I'd like to return to the house now."

It had been the oddest interchange. Upon entering the entryway, Leah moved away and walked to where her mother sat with his. Seeming to note that something was afoot, his mother stood and motioned for him to follow her to the corridor that led to the kitchens.

"Something is wrong. I can see it in yer face."

Alexander shrugged. "The lass is strange. One moment she was pleasant, speaking of the sea, the next she threatened me."

His mother's eyes widened. "Threatened?"

"I am sure she was annoyed when I told her I would nae marry her. She then stated, she could accuse me of making untoward advances and force me into it."

"I knew there was something about her I found disturbing," his mother hissed, upper lip curling. "She is sly one. Keep yer distance until they leave."

"It was a ploy for attention. When I asked if she would do it, she assured me she would nae."

"Then why bring it up?"

Alexander shook his head. "If I knew the thoughts of women, I would be a beacon for all mankind. The male sort that is."

His mother couldn't fight the smile. "She seeks a husband and is perhaps annoyed that ye are nae interested."

"It is best I keep an eye on the lass." She pressed a kiss to his cheek and returned to the great room.

Since the rain remained at bay, Alexander went to find the Grant to ask him and his sons if they would like to practice archery. If nothing else, it would keep him away from the man's daughter.

CHAPTER THIRTEEN

It was late afternoon, and Nala had managed to avoid everyone. Wishing to spend time with Sencha, they took their midday meal in the sitting room upstairs away from the others to talk privately.

In the years Nala was gone, Sencha's life had changed dramatically. Her father had died unexpectedly. A tragic accident. He'd been shot through by an errant arrow while out hunting. Then Sencha's brother had left to find his own fortune, leaving Sencha and her mother to wrestle with their home and surrounding small plot of land. Thankfully, Nala's parents had helped them, sending over their own workers to help.

Over the years, Sencha's brother had made enough to afford them more land and the ability to hire workers and servants. The house, which had fallen into disrepair had a pair of rooms added and was now a proud home.

Sencha and her mother lived alone, with visitors for company. As a result, Sencha was a lonely lass, who delighted in the company of anyone who stopped by.

"I must return home today," Sencha said, a sad expression on her face. "Knox is going on patrol near my house and has graciously offered to take me."

Nala gave her friend a knowing look. "Should I expect

anything will come of it?" Nala asked knowing Sencha had admired the handsome archer for many years. "Ye ken he is a rogue, not soon to settle."

Letting out a long breath, her friend nodded. "I am aware and remind myself that he sees me only as a friend."

"The same with Alexander," Nala said. "No matter the kisses, he will remain duty bound to the clan. He will never be mine."

Sencha looked to the doorway before speaking. "He and Leah Grant went for a walk earlier and returned arm in arm. I saw it with my own eyes. Immediately upon their entrance, Lady Ross and he went away from the room to speak. I am sure a betrothal will soon be announced. Ye must prepare yerself."

The tightening of her chest made Nala flinch. How had she allowed her feelings for him to deepen? Why hadn't she guarded her heart more? "Dinnae fret dear friend. I can take care of myself. Ye ken me, I am an independent sort."

The look Sencha gave her spoke volumes. She saw past Nala's outward expression. "I wish I could remain here. But Mother will be frantic. This is already the longest I've been away from her since…" She didn't finish the sentence as she rarely spoke of her father's passing.

Nala smiled at Sencha. "Ye care too much for the well-being of others. I will ask to return home soon. There are no prospects here for marriage. The warrior Hendry has nae sought me out again."

"What of the Grant's sons?" Sencha became animated. "They are very handsome. Perhaps the eldest, Connor. He will be laird one day and ye are a member of Clan Ross, which would be helpful in the clan's alliance."

Nala was taken aback, her eyes widening. "Do ye think Lady Ross or Alexander have considered it?"

"Perhaps. Yer father spent time speaking with Laird Grant. Yer lands do border each other's. I dare to say, yer father has in all probability considered it already."

"Oh, dear." Nala thought about it and the idea of marriage to Connor Grant would not be horrible. He was, as Sencha mentioned, very handsome.

KNOX SENT SOMEONE else to escort Sencha home, which made her friend sad and Nala angry at the man. Nonetheless, her friend seemed in good spirits as she rode away, riding with a young guard. After seeing Sencha off, Nala returned to the great room finding it empty.

"Everyone is outside watching the competition," a maid offered. It would be impolite to remain secluded, so Nala went back outside and around to the practice field.

It was an archery competition, which made it clear why Knox had not gone on patrol, since he was an archer.

"Come lass," Lady Ross called out waving her to a covered area, specially built for spectators during contests of all sorts.

Nala glanced at Leah and her mother. Only Lady Grant greeted her. Leah pretended to be engrossed in watching the men preparing to shoot their arrows.

Cynden stepped up to the line, eyed the target and shot. Everyone clapped and he bowed sweeping an arm over his head dramatically. His arrow did not hit the center of the target, which meant he would in all probability not win. It was a friendly competition as the men laughed and patted his back.

When Connor stepped to the line, he turned toward where the women sat and bowed his head, then scanned their faces. "I dedicate this winning shot to my beautiful mother."

The men shook their heads at the antics. Just then the man's blue eyes hesitated on Nala, and he gave her a wink. Nala wasn't sure it was meant for her, but then Ainslie nudged her, giggling. "The handsome man has taken notice of ye," she whispered with a grin.

As Connor turned and readied to take his shot, Nala looked over to find Alexander frowning in her direction. As she sat on the edge of the bench, next to Ainslie, it was obvious he was looking at her.

Nala let out a huff. "Is he glaring at me?" she asked Ainslie in a soft whisper. "Or is he cross with ye?"

"He must have noticed what Connor did." Ainslie clapped when the others did, and Nala followed suit although she'd not seen anything. "Ye, my dear, are the object of two men's affections it seems."

"I am nae," Nala said, unable to keep a smile from her lips.

Alexander took his turn. Unlike the others, he didn't address the spectators. He simply walked to the line and shot. His arrow was carried by a sudden gust of wind, and it plunged into the outer circle of the target.

The men roared with laughter, offering him a second try. Alexander's lips curved and he began laughing, deep dimples appearing on his cheeks. Nala did her best not to gawk at the handsome man, who she'd not seen laugh since returning. He declined the offer stating he'd still beaten Cynden.

When Knox took his turn, everyone silenced. It was well known that he was probably one of the best archers, if not the best, on the isle.

He stood straight and turned to look at Lady Ross. "Dear Aunt, who's arrow would ye like me to split?"

There was good-natured laughter as Lady Ross pretended to ponder the question. "Ye cannae split Connor's as he is our guest. I challenge ye to split Alex's arrow."

After offering a jaunty nod, the archer turned to face the target. Not taking more than a split second, he released one arrow and then a second. The first split Alexander's, the second splitting Connor's.

This time the applause was loud, everyone marveling at Knox's archery skills. He definitely was a talented archer, with eyes like those of an eagle.

"That was unbelievable," Nala said to Ainslie, who nodded in agreement.

"No matter how many times I see him in competition, his skills truly amaze me."

The contest continued and Nala became enthralled. The Grant twins were archers, and they too were very good. They elicited quite a bit of applause and cheers when taking their turns against a couple of clan Ross archers.

IT WAS HARD for Alexander to keep his attention on the competition whilst also dividing his attention between Nala and Connor. He was certain the man had made some sort of motion to Nala by her and Ainslie's reactions. Had he missed something? Perhaps Nala had an interaction with the man earlier that gave the impression she was interested in his attention.

He walked over to Knox who was still gloating over his

accomplishment and hit his cousin's shoulder. "Ye should nae have split our visitor's arrow."

Knox shrugged. "I dinnae want them to think they are better than us. I could have hit the very center of the target, that would have still beat him and his brothers."

Just then an arrow whizzed by hitting the very center of the target. A hush fell over the crowd as they searched for who had shot.

Gasps sounded as a second flew past splitting Knox's arrow.

Everything stilled as every head turned to find Nala standing with her bow lifted as she notched a third arrow. She loosed the arrow and despite a slight breeze still managed to hit the center circle of the target.

Not only had she bested the other archers, but she stood at a farther distance.

Then at the crowd's applause, she bowed theatrically. After giving her quiver and arrows to a lad who hurried over, she rejoined Ainslie and his mother.

He and Knox exchanged looks. His cousin let out a long breath. "Do ye think she is who's been the mysterious rescuer against the attackers?"

Alexander shook his head. "At the moment, I can only think that a lass just bested all the archers and am nae sure how to proceed."

NALA WAS SURE she'd just outed herself and those in the know were already sure of her role in helping the victims of the attackers. She shouldn't have done it, but it had been excruciating to remain on the sidelines and not compete.

Ainslie's wide grin and Lady Ross' compliments made her feel better. Still, she wondered if she'd overstepped by what she'd done.

"Dinnae fret," Lady Ross said seeming to read her thoughts. "Men should ken we are capable of more than stirring a pot and thrusting a needle through fabric."

"I agree," Ainslie said. "I will have to ask that ye tutor me in archery. I have done it before but am nae nearly as skilled as ye."

By the time the competition ended, it was time for last meal.

"I will order the food be served," Lady Ross said making her way down from where they sat.

"I will go with ye," Lady Grant said and turned to Leah. "Come along dear."

The women walked away, and Nala went to follow, but Ainslie held her back. "Someone wishes to speak to ye."

Nala allowed Ainslie to tug her to the side of the tent, then stood confused when Ainslie sauntered away. There was no one heading in her direction. The Grant and his sons were in conversation with Knox and Cynden.

"A word," Alexander said taking her arm and guiding her away from the others. They didn't stop walking until reaching the side garden.

"I can explain," Nala said, expecting to be admonished.

Instead of answering, he asked a question. "Have ye spoken to Connor Grant? It seems ye have garnered his attention."

Surprised at the direction of his question, Nala was confused. "I am nae opposed to marrying him," Nala blurted.

"Our lands border and Father seemed to like the laird."

For a long moment, Alexander stared at her, as if at a loss for words. Neither did he seem angry or glad, his expression gave away nothing.

Nala had to break the silence. "I had nae heard ye laugh since I returned. It was good to see ye in good spirits during the archery challenge."

The muscle on the side of his face, at the jawline, twitched. He was grinding his teeth. Obviously he wasn't happy with her.

"Say something," Nala said. "Are ye cross with me about my participating in the competition without being invited?"

"Of course not, why would I be?" Alexander replied. "I knew ye were good, but I was nae aware of how precise yer shooting is. It will be good to ken ye can defend me if the need arises."

She fought the urge to grin and hug him. "Ye wished to speak to me. What is it that ye wanted to talk to me about?"

Alexander's brow fell into a frown, his eyes searching her face. In that moment, the thought of their shared kisses and the one intimate moment flashed in her mind. She ached to reach out, to kiss and caress him.

"The archer…" Alexander began.

Nala's stomach sank. If he asked if she was the mysterious archer who rescued people, he'd probably tell her parents. It would mean her freedom would definitely be taken from her.

"I came to fetch ye. Yer mother wishes for us to join her for honeyed mead in the parlor," Leah interrupted threading her arm through Alexander's. She gave Nala a flat look. "Ye too, I suppose."

Despite wishing to storm away from them, Nala forced a soft smile. "It will be my pleasure."

Leah's eyebrows rose when Nala joined them walking on the opposite side of Alexander.

"May I inquire why ye are here?" Leah said, peering at Nala. "Do ye not have a home?"

"Nala and I have known each other since childhood," Alexander replied in a curt tone. Nala wasn't sure if he was more annoyed with her or Leah. She guessed it was herself.

He continued, "Our families are very close."

"I am here to visit," Nala interjected. "To become reacquainted with the Ross family after being gone to England for ten years."

Leah gave a soft huff. "Strange that ye didnae marry after so many seasons in England. It is rare for a woman to be alone at yer age."

If not for the barrier of Alexander between them, Nala would have yanked the woman by the hair and slapped her silly.

"It was my choice. English men cannae compare to Scottish men. They are soft and pampered," Nala replied truthfully.

Alexander turned and gave her an amused look and then addressed Leah. "Would ye consider yer brothers to be pampered, Leah?"

"Of course not," Leah retorted. "They are warriors through and through. Of good stock like all of the Grant clan's men."

Once again he directed a glance to Nala. "Ye must be relieved to hear that."

"What do ye mean by that?" Leah asked stopping. "Why

would *she* be relieved?" she asked.

Neither Alexander nor Nala replied. Instead, he motioned for Leah to enter the house. Then Nala—who pretended to stumble—promptly stomped on his foot.

When he grunted, she gave him an innocent look. "I apologize, Laird".

Throughout the entire meal, Alexander ignored everyone but the visiting laird. Nala kept an eye on Leah wondering what the woman planned to do after the meal. She'd probably come up with a reason to get him alone so they could discuss their betrothal and perhaps even kiss him.

The more Nala considered it, the angrier she got. It wasn't her place to be upset. Nothing could be done about the fact that thoughts of them hurt. Somehow she had to take control of her emotions. Things like this were bound to happen, she'd always known Alexander would only marry for the benefit of the clan.

Nala leaned over to speak to Lady Ross. "I am going to seek my bed. I feel a bit tired."

"Of course lass," Lady Ross looked at her with curiosity. "Would ye like me to send a maid up with some warm cider perhaps?"

What she needed was to be left alone. Nala shook her head. "I see one now. I will ask her myself. Thank ye."

After bidding a good night to Lady Grant and Leah, who looked her up and down and then turned to look where Alexander spoke to Laird Grant.

In her bedchamber, Nala stalked from one side to the other until a knock on her door startled her. She opened it to find a chambermaid who ushered in two red-faced lads carrying a wooden tub. "Lady Ross asked that we bring ye a bath to help soothe ye."

A warm bath would surely help, Nala thought as she moved aside to allow more maids with buckets of water to enter.

It was much later that she climbed out of the bath. She'd told the maids to wait until the next day to come for it. That way she could stay in as long as possible.

Standing before the hearth, the coolness of the room brought shivers. What was Alexander doing at the moment? Was he with Leah? What if… She turned away from the fire, exasperated at the direction of her thoughts and pulled on her nightshift.

It was best to climb into her bed and try to sleep.

Nala brushed her damp hair, taming the curls with practiced twisting as she bent before the fire so that the heat would help it dry.

Her gaze kept going to the door.

Alexander would never be hers. The sooner she accepted it, the better.

CHAPTER FOURTEEN

Outside his window, the starlit sky was astonishingly beautiful that night. With only a tartan around his recently bathed body, and bare feet upon the cold stone floor, Alexander shivered.

After one last long look up at the sky, he closed the shutters and walked to stand in front of the hearth, the fire warming his cooled body.

Thoughts whirled at all that had happened that day and he absently reached for his glass of whiskey to drink. The amber liquid left a trail of warmth as it moved down his body.

It had been an eventful day, tomorrow the Grants would leave after having formed a bond between them.

Thankfully, the Grant had not insisted that Alexander consider marriage but had good-naturedly agreed to the terms the Ross council and he had discussed thoroughly. All in all, it had been a good visit and a perfect way to wrap things up after the long seasons of chaos and fighting that his clan had suffered.

After folding the tartan over the foot of the bed, Alexander slid between the blankets waiting for the inevitable warmth to lull him to sleep.

THE BÌRLINN SWAYED *haphazardly. The vessel taking on water* whilst the sea tossed it about. His shoulder hit the side of the boat, and he swore.

How was he there?

"Alex. Alex." *Nala was there? They were in danger. Somehow he had to warn her. It was so dark that he had to rely on her voice to find her.*

"Alex."

Alex sat up with a start and looked about the darkness for a moment, some of the shadows looked familiar. Was he still dreaming?

Movement beside the bed made him lunge toward it, grabbing the person and pulling them down face-first onto the bed.

It was a woman, and by her plump bottom that he was pressed against, she wore only nightclothes.

"What are ye doing here?"

Whatever she said was unintelligible, since her face was pressed into the bedding. Finally, she turned her head sideways. "Let me up, ye idiot."

"Nala?" He released her and she scrambled to stand beside the bed, pushing her hair back from her face. "Was that necessary?"

"Ye cannae walk into someone's bedchamber in the dead of night and not expect to be confronted."

"Attacked," she stated, her pretty face now lit by the dwindling embers in the hearth. "Why would ye attack someone who tries to wake ye."

"I thought I was in a bìrlinn." At her perplexed expression, he asked, "Is something wrong?"

She gave him an impatient look. "Will ye marry her?"

"Ye came here to wake me and ask if I am marrying someone?" Alexander pretended to be mad while wondering how long it would take Nala to realize he was bare as the day he was born.

"Will ye be marrying Connor Grant?"

"That is neither here nor there. I asked ye a question first," the stubborn lass said, crossing her arms. "Well?" she added with a tap of her bare foot.

"Ye do realize it is a cool night. Ye have no shoes and I, well, I am missing a lot more than just shoes."

First she looked him up and down, then her mouth fell open. She went to take a step, but instead fell backward onto the bed and sat. The result was that her face was level with his sex.

"Oh goodness," Nala covered her face. "Why are ye naked?" she asked, face still covered.

"I often sleep bereft of clothes," Alexander replied. "That is why I keep a tartan on the foot of my bed."

"Put something on," she hissed.

He took his time walking to fetch said item, then wrapped it and deftly secured it at his waist. Although the cloth fell just past his knees, it left most of his upper body vulnerable to the coolness of the room.

"Ye can look now," Alexander said unsure he wanted Nala to move away from his bed. He'd pictured her there several times, and each time it had ended with him having to take himself in hand.

He'd finally accepted that the woman aroused him like no other. Even then, his staff began to harden.

"What, pray tell, is so important it brought ye to seek me

whilst I slept?"

Her eyes flickered to his face, then down his body, as if assessing if he was truly dressed. Alexander did his best not to smile. Despite her protests, and asking that he dress, there had been desire when taking him in. There was no doubt in his mind, Nala was there because she wanted him. Whether she admitted it to him or herself was something he'd like to know.

"I asked if ye plan to marry Leah. Ye didnae reply."

In three strides, he closed the distance between them. "I have nae decided." In truth, he doubted he'd ever marry the lass. He'd not considered them to be compatible.

Nala took him in. "It is either aye or nae. How hard can it be?" She looked up to the ceiling. "I am sure ye ken what ye plan to do."

It would be easy to say that he'd already decided not to marry Leah; however, this interchange was quite enjoyable. He wanted to see how far Nala would push.

"Ye didnae answer my question either," Alexander stated. "Will ye marry the Grant's son?"

Nala's shoulders lifted and lowered. "The decision will be made by my father and yerself. I have little say."

"Do ye wish to?" Alexander hated asking because her reply had the potential to hurt. Somehow he managed to keep a neutral expression.

"I have nae decided," the fiery wench replied. "I see this was a waste of time. I best return to bed." She turned away and took a pair of steps before Alexander stopped her.

"I can make whatever ye want to happen. If ye wish to marry him, all ye have to do is ask."

Nala turned and glared up at him. "Of course ye can. Ye

have my fate in the palm of yer hand."

"Why are ye so angry? It is the way of things. At least I am giving ye a choice."

"I am angry because I dinnae truly have a choice. Because no matter what I say, it will not matter in the end. If Father decides that I will marry someone old enough to be my father, or the stinky cobbler from the village, that is what I must do."

Alexander wrinkled his nose. "The cobber is stinky?"

Obviously it was the wrong time to joke, because Nala threw herself at him, hands balled into fists and face contorted with rage she hit his chest.

Caught off guard, Alexander stumbled. Stepping on the edge of his tartan, he lost his balance and fell backward. In his effort not to fall, he grabbed Nala. They hit the floor, Nala landing hard on his stomach knocking the wind out of him. Not wishing to allow her to gain an advantage Alexander held her atop him. It was possible the vexed lass would kick him if she stood up and he was still on the floor.

"Let me go!" Nala hissed, struggling. "Surely someone heard the noise ye made and will arrive shortly."

Alexander met her gaze. "Ye want to ken what I think?"

She slid a look sideways. "Not really."

It wasn't a *no*, so he continued, "I think ye want me. Ye cannae stand the thought of me with another. Ye are angry because ye cannae except that ye are in love with me."

Nala struggled to free herself from his grasp, but Alexander held her firm. "Tell me I am wrong. Kiss me Nala to prove me right."

The words seemed to take the fight out of Nala, and her wide eyes met his for a moment before moving to his mouth.

Seeming to catch herself, she jerked her gaze back up.

"I will dinnae such thing."

"Kiss me."

Again she hesitated, but the hunger in her eyes was palpable. Finally, Nala let out a soft breath and to his delight her mouth crashed over his, taking him with so much fervor, his eyes fell closed and at once the coldness of the stone flooring didn't bother him one bit.

Releasing her hands, Alexander slid his up and down her sides, until stopping at her round delicious bottom and palming it. He pulled her against his hardness, and she gasped at the realization of how she'd affected him.

She was inexperienced, but it mattered little because never before had Alexander felt so disarmed as he did in that moment.

Trailing his lips up her neck, reaching her earlobe, he nibbled it gently. Nala let out the softest of moans.

Once again he took her mouth, her plump lips parting for him. He loved the delicious way she responded with eagerness.

His hardness pulsed demanding more. "Ye should leave Nala. There is only so much control I can have."

For a moment she stilled and then lowered her head onto his chest. Having her in his arms felt right. Perfect even.

"I dinnae wish to leave."

A burst of relief filled him. He wrapped his arms around her and holding onto her tightly he rolled them both over so that he could take her mouth again. The kiss was different this time, her fingers threading through his hair. Again her lips parted, and he delved into the sweet taste of her, their tongues twisting in the erotic dance of lovers.

He broke the kiss and looked into her eyes. "Nala," Alexander whispered, "I have thought about ye here in my bed so many times."

Eyes soft, lips swollen, a dreamy expression, how was it possible for her to be more beautiful? "I have thought about ye as well," she replied. "Kiss me, Alex."

He loved it when she used his shortened name, and it was like a caress over his heated skin.

He picked her up and carried her to his bed, then Alexander took her mouth, running his hands up her legs, pushing her nightshift up and up until she was bare from the waist down.

The touching of skin against skin sent shivers up them both. Nala released a soft sound much like a happy kitten when he trailed kisses from her neck. He pushed the nightshift further up, exposing her beautiful breasts. They were not big, nor small, but perfectly proportion. The tan tips pert, inviting him to partake.

He finished undressing her, pulling the cumbersome piece of clothing over her head. Nala didn't shirk or try to cover herself when he admired the view of her beautiful body.

"Tell me to stop at any time and I will," Alexander said while kissing her lips. He then lowered to pay homage to each breast, sucking each tip into his mouth, teasing the tiny buds with his tongue. The whole while Nala squirmed, her legs sliding up and down, as she tried in vain to quelch the feeling.

"I feel as if on fire," she rasped. "What is it?"

"Arousal," Alexander replied. "Allow it to flow through ye. Dinnae fight it." He peered down at her.

Sliding his fingers up her thigh she stilled and arched her

back in anticipation. "I-I want more… please."

Of course this wasn't his first time with a woman, but for some reason it felt so new, so very different. Alexander wanted to relish each second, to ensure Nala was fully satisfied and sated by the time it was over.

When she ran her hands down his back, exploring his body, her touch was bolder than he would have expected. Not hesitant in the least. Nala's lips curved. "I expected that ye would have a lovely body."

Pride filled him and he was glad to have taken care with bathing earlier. "Ye do as well."

She looked up at him, eyes half closed. "The pull between us is strong. I cannae deny ye anything right now."

At the invitation, he moved further up her leg until his fingers reached her sex and he slid them between the folds. Heat and wetness met his touch and Nala arched into his hand. Splaying her apart, Alexander circled the nub with the pad of one finger and Nala gasped.

Eyes closed and lips parted, she urged him to continue.

Her panting against his ear was so sensual his already hard cock was becoming like stone. He wanted her more than anything, and he was losing control of his senses.

"Augh!" Nala came undone, shuddering as she found release. Her nails dug into his shoulders, and she kissed his neck, suckling just beneath his jaw.

"I want more," she whispered.

"Nala, are ye sure?" Alexander's words were hoarse as he fought to maintain control. "Ye should go, now. I cannae keep myself from taking ye."

He started to roll away, but she clung to him as her life

depended on it. "Nae. I want ye to be my first. I want to experience this only with ye."

His sex responded, throbbing with need and he let out a long breath. Wild horses could not stop what was about to happen.

His reasoning fled, and all he knew was that the woman in his bed would be his and no one else's. His fate was sealed, and he didn't resent it one bit.

Taking her mouth once again, Alexander positioned himself over her, then he guided himself to her entrance.

Nala trailed kisses from his mouth to his jaw and then down his neck as he moved up so that they were aligned.

She remained so wet, he almost came when the tip of his cock came in contact with her sex.

It was a battle to keep from thrusting fully into her. It was her first experience, so he was forced to be gentle.

Nala pushed her head back against the bedding, not seeming at all nervous. Instead, there was a soft smile on her lips, and she grasped his bottom.

Inch by inch, he entered her. Then upon feeling her maidenhead, he took her mouth and slipped his tongue between her lips. She kissed him passionately, her hands gliding up his back. Alexander nipped her tongue gently as he thrust into her.

She stiffened and gasped a slight frown marring her beauty.

"It only happens once. It will pass," Alexander whispered into her ear.

After a moment she relaxed, her eyes meeting his with so much trust, he wanted to hold her forever. However, his throbbing cock demanded attention. He began to move slowly, in and out in a steady rhythm.

It was only moments before Nala's mouth fell open, her breathing jagged as she began to ascend, her body responding to his movements.

Eyes shut, she moaned loudly making his heart swell. His fiery lass was made for lovemaking. It didn't surprise him in the least.

Alexander slid his hand beneath her and lifted her so he could take her fully and plunged into her, barely able to keep from spilling at the sight of the beauty beneath him.

His entire body shook when he didn't allow himself release, wanting her to come first. Lowering her, he bent and took her mouth again, kissing her until she panted.

"Oh!" Nala arched her back and shuddered as she climaxed.

Finally Alexander allowed his own body free rein, and he came with so much force he had to push his face into the bedding to muffle his moans.

His body trembled, hips pushing into Nala as he lost all control. Stars burst behind his lids and the room spun round and round as he grasped Nala tightly waiting for the rush of his release to pass.

Whatever this was, it had never happened before.

Alexander collapsed over Nala, his harsh breathing matching hers.

"I am crushing ye," Alexander said a moment later, his voice breathless as he rolled to his side bringing her against him.

"I didnae mind," she whispered and pressed a kiss on his chest.

"I was nae sure what to expect," Nala said breathlessly. "It is wonderful. Ye are wonderful."

A chuckle escaped. "With ye, aye."

She let out a sigh and soon her breathing steadied as she fell asleep.

A smile lingering on his lips Alexander allowed sleep to take him as well.

CHAPTER FIFTEEN

Nala woke with a start. The unfamiliar surroundings making her rub her eyes to ensure she was indeed awake. Everything was different. The large bed, thick bedding over her, and next to her someone slept.

Ever so slowly, she turned her head to see who it was. Thankfully, there was enough sunlight slipping through the cracks of the shutters that the room was not entirely dark. Alexander was fast asleep, facing her.

When her heart began to thunder, Nala worried it was loud enough to wake him. She'd spent the night there.

Not only that. She'd given herself to him. Her mind whirled and she had to take several deep breaths before she could calm herself enough to think straight.

Tentatively, she reached under to blanket and sure enough, she was bereft of clothing, bare as a bairn. He was probably the same. He'd nae been wearing anything when she'd come into the room.

What had she been thinking? Of course a man would take a woman coming to him in the middle of the night as an invitation for a dalliance.

Nala had to be honest with herself. Alexander had not taken advantage of the situation, as a matter of fact, he had not only told her to leave but had asked several times if she was sure. Too overcome with passion, she had not wanted what was happening to end.

At a soft snore, she held her breath. He didn't wake, his face was lax in slumber. His lips parted, eyes closed, the dark lashes fanning down atop his cheekbones. The man was breathtaking.

Alexander had been hers and she had been completely his. Their lovemaking had been the most wonderful experience of her life.

Now, however, she had to leave. Escape before he awakened because she wasn't sure what to say to him.

Would he think she'd come there in order to trap him into marriage? Worse yet, that he would insist they marry solely because of the interlude. She could never do it, force a man to marry her against his wishes, or out of duty.

Nala slid sideways, slowly, inch by inch until her left leg fell from the bed and her foot found purchase. Then she sat up, ensuring to keep the blankets over Alexander until she finally slipped fully from the bed.

After tiptoeing to where her nightshift was discarded, she quickly pulled it over her head and dashed to the door. One last glance to the bed to be certain he continued sleeping confirmed it. He slept soundly.

Nala opened the door and slipped out into the corridor and then ran toward her bedchamber. She turned a corner and ran into a broad chest. Her breath caught and she stumbled backward. Thankfully, the large man was able to catch her by the arms to keep her from falling onto the floor.

"Why are ye running down corridors?" Cynden's hazel gaze studied her. "Is something wrong?"

"Nae," Nala replied breathlessly. "I came from the water closet and got confused finding my way back to my bedchamber. Now I am utterly lost."

His brow creased. Nala was not only in the wrong corridor, but on the wrong floor. But he seemed to believe her. "Go down there,"—he pointed to a stairway—"and up to the next floor. Yer bedchamber is on the left."

"Oh, thank ye." Nala hurried away, not giving him the opportunity to ask more questions.

Once in her bedchamber, she collapsed onto the bed and rolled onto her stomach before pushing her face into the bedding and screaming.

What had she done?

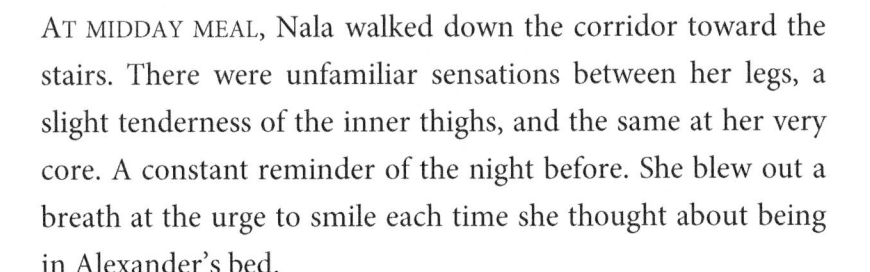

AT MIDDAY MEAL, Nala walked down the corridor toward the stairs. There were unfamiliar sensations between her legs, a slight tenderness of the inner thighs, and the same at her very core. A constant reminder of the night before. She blew out a breath at the urge to smile each time she thought about being in Alexander's bed.

She'd purposely skipped first meal, hoping that he'd gone by the time she came down. Her stomach had been making loud noises for a while in protest of the missed meal. Upon entering the great room, Nala made her way quickly to the table where Lady Ross and Ainslie were. Both greeted her fondly.

"Ye missed first meal," Lady Ross said. "Were ye feeling poorly this morning?"

Nala wanted to curse the heat at her cheeks. "A bit, aye. But I feel much better now." She reached for the loaf of bread and sliced a thick piece off, then slathered it liberally with butter. Atop it, she piled thinly sliced lamb and cheese.

Her mouth watered in anticipation. Just as she was about to take a bit, Alexander walked up to their table. "Can I have a word with ye, Nala?"

Lady Ross chuckled. "She looks about to cry. Allow the lass to have her meal, she missed first meal."

"It will be but a moment," Alexander insisted.

Nala gave Lady Ross a grateful look, then took the biggest bite she could of her delicious creation before standing.

"What is it?" she purposely asked in front of the ladies in hopes they wouldn't suspect something happened between them.

Without a reply, he took her elbow and guided her from the room. They walked to his study and once inside, he closed the door.

"How are ye faring? I was worried when I didnae see ye at first meal." His dark gaze took her in from head to toe.

This was a new Alexander, one she never would have expected. Had he always been so attentive to her? No, she didn't think so.

She lifted her chin and gave him what she hoped was a steady gaze. Although of their own volition, her eyes moved to his lips for a split second. "I am well. No need to fash yerself."

"Nala, we must discuss things." He shook his head. "I will make things right."

"What things?" Nala looked up at him. "Dinnae feel as if ye owe me anything. I allowed things to progress because I wanted it to happen. We are adults and capable of doing what we wish."

"What of repercussions? Have ye considered that?" The familiar annoyed tone she was used to came out as he directed a pointed look to her midsection.

Nala shrugged. "If it comes to be then we can decide then. I dinnae plan to change my life because of ye." It was true, the last thing she wanted was to force him into marriage. If he wanted to feel better about their interlude by appearing concerned, she'd not take it away from him.

"I am very hungry and would like to return to my meal before someone else descends upon it." Nala rounded him and before he could stop her, she hurried back to her meal.

Men were certainly interesting creatures. They pretended to be detached when in her experience, they were as sentimental about some things as women were.

When she returned to the table, she ate the bread and then prepared another. It was obvious both her companions wished to know what Alexander wanted to talk about, but Nala couldn't come up with a believable topic.

Finally Lady Ross spoke. "Alexander is nae going to marry the Grant lass. Is that what he wished to assure ye about?"

Nala had forgotten about the woman. "Oh…aye, in a way. Although I am nae sure why he wishes me to ken that."

Ainslie and Lady Ross exchanged amused looks. "Both of ye need to admit that ye are attracted to one another," Ainslie said with an exaggerated huff. "It is obvious to the entire world."

A laugh escaped and Nala grinned. "To the entire world? I sincerely doubt the world is engaged in what happens inside the keep. We are childhood friends. I admit loving him because of it. I dinnae think it is nothing more."

"Then a betrothal with the Grant lass would nae bother ye?" Lady Ross asked. "If that is so, it would be a benefit to the clan. Perhaps I can arrange a visit," she finished.

Bread halfway to her mouth, Nala froze. Was that it? If she didn't admit to wanting Alexander, he would be married to the twit, Leah? The woman would never make him happy, he deserved someone better than the bland redhead.

"Why her? She is as bland as a dry piece of stale bread. He should marry someone fiery. A woman who will stand up to him and stand up for him. Alexander should marry someone strong and gentle at the same time. A woman who will be a true laird's wife, willing to assist in clan matters."

Letting out a breath, she took another bite of her food.

"Where can I find such a woman?" Lady Grant looked to Ainslie. "Do ye ken someone like whom Nala described?"

Ainslie grinned and grasped her hands in front of her chest. "Aye, I do. How have I nae seen it sooner?"

Nala waited to hear the name of the woman, both seemed to realize would be perfect, but they didn't say anything more.

Just as she was about to ask, a guard rushed into the room and over to where Alexander was. He stood and they hurried from the room.

"Let us pray it has nothing to do with another case of attackers," Lady Ross said looking in the direction the men had gone.

It was a long moment before Cynden came to where they sat. "Mother, there is naught to worry about. Just an argument at the village. Two men fighting over a lass, one pulled a knife and cut the other. Then others became involved. Alexander's presence is required."

Lady Ross stood and motioned to Nala and Ainslie. "I will go to the village as well. Ainslie, ye should remain here. Nala would ye come with me?"

"Of course," Nala said sliding a look to a disappointed Ainslie. "I will listen intently and tell ye all upon my return."

"Very well," Ainslie replied, seeming a bit mollified.

As they rode toward the village in a coach, Nala ventured to ask, "Why could Ainslie nae come?"

"As she is with child. She does nae need to be exposed to conflict. One never knows what might happen."

Nala frowned. "Why do ye wish to go then?"

"If there is a woman involved, she will need either scolding for leading two men on, or comfort if caught in something not of her doing."

It wasn't much later that they arrived at the village. The square was crowded with onlookers, so it was hard to see if anything happened.

"Come," Lady Ross instructed hurrying to the seamstress shop. There was no one inside the shop, which didn't slow Lady Ross as she rushed past the empty space to a set of stairs. They went up the stairs and into a small sitting room. There the seamstress and her helper stood by the windows.

The lady turned and smiled at Lady Ross. "Come and see. The two idiots were pulled apart, but they are nae happy. Cormac is bleeding like a stuck pig, whilst Athol has a broken nose."

Nala went to the window that had a clear view of the village square.

People were shouting over each other, everyone seeming to be taking sides. An older woman had rushed to the man who was bleeding and struggled to wrap his arm while he fought against the men who held him.

The other man, Athol, yelled and pointed his knife at Cormac, blood was smeared from his nose across his cheek where he'd obviously wiped at it.

"Who is the woman they fight over?" Lady Ross asked, her gaze never leaving the scene below.

"Angus MacLean's eldest, Ila," the seamstress replied. "She is betrothed to Cormac, but apparently was caught kissing Athol."

Lady Ross leaned out the window peering in both directions. "Where is the lass?"

"Over there by the tavern, ye cannae see her from here." Came the seamstress' reply.

They watched as the crowd parted and Alexander walked over to stand between the two men. Nala couldn't help but admire how he stood out from the other men. His commanding presence brought the entire crowd to silence.

Turning to the people gathered, he glowered. "Instead of encouraging this, ye should be taking care of yer own."

There were soft murmurs and some of the people walked away. There would be nothing more of interest to see. The men would not fight in the laird's presence. Whatever the issue was, it would be settled by talking.

Surrounded by guards, the two men were ushered into the tavern.

Nala caught sight of a young woman near the tavern. She was crying into her hands, two men at her side.

"There she is," the seamstress said. "Her brothers dinnae look pleased at her antics. Oh to be a fly on the wall."

Lady Ross motioned to Nala. "Come, let us go speak to her." She turned to the seamstress. "I will tell ye what happens, Orla."

The woman smiled and turned back to the window.

THEY CROSSED THE road toward the tavern where the woman, Ila, remained. She'd stopped crying and seemed to have accepted that she would have to wait to hear her fate from the laird.

Upon Lady Ross' approach, the two men acknowledged her with mumbled greetings, their ire apparent.

"Go inside and see about what is said," Lady Ross said. "I will remain here with Ila."

The brothers gave their sister a withering look and hurried inside.

Ila gave Lady Ross a stricken look, tears streaming down her face. "I will be considered the village tart. I dinnae mean for it to happen. But it is my fault. I kissed Athol."

"Why did ye kiss him?" Nala asked.

Ila glanced at her, it was as if she'd not noticed Nala until then. "Oh, I remember ye. Do ye remember that we used to go to the creek and try to catch wee fish?"

At once the memory of spending days with Ila came to her. "Aye, I do remember now."

With a big sigh, Ila shook her head. "My brothers want me to marry Cormac, but I dinnae want to. I have always loved

Athol."

"Why will they nae allow it? For ye to marry Athol?" Lady Ross asked.

"They dinnae like that he is a sheep herder. Claim he cannae provide well for me and any bairns to come."

Lady Ross began reassuring Ila, while Nala's mind went back to earlier in the great room. Was she doomed to marry someone she didn't care for because Alexander would marry this woman Ainslie thought to be perfect?

Something burned in her chest, and she flattened her hand over the spot. Was she in love with Alexander? If so, when had it happened? It had to be true. Otherwise, why would it hurt physically to think of him with someone else?

Nala stood and stretched, unable to hear whatever it was the two women discussed. Her mind returned to the night before. It had not been Alexander's first time with a woman, of that she had no doubt. And although she'd experienced stolen kisses with men whilst living in England, she'd never allowed anyone the liberty of anything more.

Had being with her meant as much to Alexander? Nala could ask, but she wasn't sure she was prepared for his answer. If he dismissed it as nothing more than an enjoyable liaison, it would shatter her.

IT WAS A while later that one of Ila's brothers emerged. He glanced at Lady Ross and then to his sister. By his murderous expression, things had not gone as he'd wished. "The laird requests that ye come inside."

Nala walked behind Lady Ross and Ila into the room. The poor lass shook visibly, her gaze downcast.

"Ila," Alexander said, his voice even. "Ye will marry one of the two men. I leave the decision up to ye, but it will happen today."

Ila gasped, her widened eyes meeting Alexander's before going directly to Athol, whose nose had stopped bleeding but had purpling appearing around his left eye.

"I wish to marry Athol," Ila said in a firm tone. "I love him."

The other man Cormac started to say something, but at a warning look from Alexander, he stopped himself and let out an angry huff.

"Very well," Alexander said, then addressed her brothers. "Ye will support them in whatever they require. Ensure that yer sister is well provided for. Ye have the resources to help with a cottage and seed money."

The brothers looked at each other and then nodded in agreement. "Aye, Laird," one replied. By the glances of worry toward their sister, they did care for her.

"Go fetch the vicar," Alexander said to a guard who left immediately.

"Should we celebrate with a pint?" Alexander motioned to the barkeep. "I will pay for everyone's first drink."

All seemed to be forgotten. Even Cormac rushed to get his tankard and then shuffled to a table where he was soon surrounded by—who Nala surmised—were his supporters.

THE HARRIED VICAR arrived, looking worse for wear. Nala felt for the older man who looked as if he'd rather be anywhere other than inside a tavern in the middle of the day. The clergy proceeded to ask the couple to stand before him, his gaze traveling several times to where the barkeep stood. The tavern was not exactly a place a vicar probably visited often and surely had never conducted a wedding ceremony there.

Or perhaps it was that he was thirsty and hoped for a drink, Nala considered.

As the ceremony began, the vicar's words floated over the now silent crowd. Nala lifted her gaze across the room to where Alexander stood.

There was something odd about his expression when he met her eyes. A warmth, or perhaps it was the recollection of the night before. Her heartbeat quickened and she had to take a deep breath. Tearing her eyes from his, she turned her attention back to the ceremony. Ila beamed with happiness and despite the lingering blood droplets on his tunic and purpling eye, Athol looked to be happy as well.

The vicar finally finished with a blessing after the exchange of vows and the couple was engulfed in hugs and claps on the back in Athol's case. Even a sulky Cormac went forward to congratulate the couple.

"What do ye think?" Alexander had come up behind her making Nala start.

She didn't look up at him. "Ye did well."

The touch of his hand on the small of her back sent shivers of awareness through her. If only she could lean back into him, have his arms around her.

"Ye and Mother should return to the keep. There is still restlessness in the village. I prefer for both of ye to be safe."

Lady Ross turned to look at her son. "I will stop at the square to purchase a few things. We have two guards with us. I am sure all will be fine." She took Alexander's arm. "Walk us out, dear."

To Nala's consternation, he kept his hand on the small of her back as he directed them to the doorway. It was difficult to keep from touching him in return.

It was heavenly when he pulled her closer as they went through the doorway, tucking her against his side.

Nala almost closed her eyes, but the brightness of the day outside brought her reason back and she stepped away.

CHAPTER SIXTEEN

ALEXANDER SAT IN the tavern with Knox and another pair of guards. The wedding party had gone leaving only them and a group of men at a table by the doorway.

After emptying his tankard, he placed it on the surface before the barkeep. "One more Angus."

The burly man promptly took the tankard and refilled it from a pitcher. "There ye are, Laird."

"There seems to be something on yer mind," Knox said interrupting his thoughts. He'd been considering whether or not it was a good idea to ask Nala to join him in bed again that night.

She'd probably rebuff him. The more times he lay with her, the greater the chances of producing a bairn. He would never sire a child out of wedlock. No child of his would be born a bastard.

"I am considering something. One way or another, both alternatives are nae good."

Knox shook his head. "Then forget about whatever it is. Ye have enough to worry about without adding a new problem to yer life."

"Ye are right," Alexander replied. "That is what I should do."

The reply from Knox was a bland look. "Ah, ye are going

to do one or the other. Ye will make a mistake."

Alexander looked to the ceiling. Was he going to dive into something deeper with Nala? Could he walk away?

The entire ride back to the keep, his mind kept going back to the night before. It would be impossible to attend to his responsibilities if he couldn't concentrate on matters at hand.

Alexander shook his head in an attempt to dislodge thoughts of the beautiful woman who'd been in his bed. Never had he beheld such a woman, from her smooth skin the color of an autumn leaf to her perfect shapely legs, rounded hips, and pert breasts. She was someone he could never tire of sharing his bed with.

Was this what happened to his brothers? Is this why their heads stopped turning when a bonny lass was in sight? He couldn't think of any woman getting his attention, not as long as Nala was his.

The thought was as terrifying as it was alluring. To share his bed with her night after night, to awaken to the sight of her.

At the last thought, he frowned. She'd slipped out without waking him. He woke up and reached to her only to find the space beside him empty. The sprite had escaped taking with her an opportunity for morning time together.

The keep came into sight, and he studied the proud structure. His home, and the gathering place for Clan Ross. Now all he had to do was to consider what to do about Nala. He'd speak to her first and gauge her thoughts on marriage. Nae, not on marriage. Her thoughts about marrying him.

His stomach lurched at the idea. Tying himself to a woman was not something he'd ever thought of as something he'd wish to do. Alexander let out a slow breath. Was he ready for such a commitment?

ONCE THE HORSES were taken away, Alexander walked toward the main house. Cynden stood outside with a man who climbed onto the bench of his wagon and headed toward the gates.

"Who was that?" Alexander asked upon nearing his brother.

"He came to ask to be considered for providing hogs next season," Cynden replied and then cocked his head to the side and studied Alexander. "There is something different about ye." His brother's lips quivered as if he fought laughter.

Alexander ran his hands down his face and studied his palms. Other than dirt, there wasn't anything on his face. "What do ye mean?"

"I saw something very curious this morn." Cynden gave him a pointed look and then glanced over his shoulder looking to the upper levels of the house. "In the corridor."

Unsure what his brother went on about, Alexander gave him a droll look. "A wee ghosty scared ye?"

"No, I saw a beautiful lass hurrying away from yer bedchamber. She ran into me. Looked every bit like a lassie who'd been recently ravaged."

For a moment Alexander wasn't sure what to say. He grabbed Cynden's arm and pulled him to the side garden. "What happened exactly?"

"Just what I said," Cynden was obviously enjoying the

situation. "I was walking back from the kitchens to bring Ainslie cider when the lass practically ran me over. She said to be lost and then hurried away."

His brother grinned. "She was nae lost, was she?"

"Dinnae say anything about it." Alexander paced. "I have to decide what I must do. Nae, I ken what I must do. It is just that…" He raked his fingers through his hair.

"The idea of marriage terrifies ye," Cynden finished for him. "I dinnae ken why. It is past time, Alex."

Retracing his steps, Alexander blew out a harsh breath. "I must marry her. I cannae take her maidenhood and not. It is the right thing to do."

There was a rustling sound as if something or someone hurried away. Both he and Cynden turned but didn't see anything.

"Probably scared a hare with all yer ramblings," Cynden said turning his attention back to Alexander. "Do ye not care for her?"

"I can think of nothing else but Nala. I believe to be bewitched." Alexander shook his head. "But marriage—"

Cynden interrupted, "What scares ye brother? The idea of nae having another woman once ye are married? Or the idea of being tied down?"

"I am nae scared. What if what we feel for each other is nae enough? What if she does nae wish to marry me? What will happen if there is nae love, ever?"

"How do ye feel when thinking of Nala?"

It was as if the burden on his shoulders lightened. "Everything about her is perfect. Have ye ever seen such a beautiful shade as her skin? I think of her independent nature and am enthralled. Her archery skills are enviable. The way she responded to my touch… I care for her and cannae imagine Nala with another."

Cynden placed his palm on Alexander's shoulder. "Sounds like ye are well on yer way to love. I pity any man that tries to come between ye and the bonny lass."

Just the thought quickened his heart. "Perhaps ye are right."

His brother looked toward the interior of the house. "There are a few more people waiting to be heard," Cynden said. "I came out to get a breath of air. Today those who've come to seek an audience with ye have mostly had arguments that have taken all my patience. But if ye wish to seek out Nala, I can continue to take yer place."

Alexander shook his head. "Nay. I need time to consider everything. I will address the rest of those inside."

There was a look of relief on Cynden's face. The duties of a laird were many and at times Alexander himself had a hard time not losing his temper. For the most part, he enjoyed helping the clan's people, but he agreed with Cynden that it could be draining.

"Laird." A man walked up when he entered. "I am next." He motioned to a man who stood ramrod straight in front of the high board. "He thinks to be first because he stands there. I was in the front but had to go to the privy."

He looked at the man before him. "What do ye wish to speak to me about? Ye are in front of me, have my attention, ye could have stated whatever it is by now."

The man blinked up at him. "Oh, aye, Laird. I came to ask

for a larger portion of land so I can plant more and therefore have more to provide the clan."

Alexander knew the man to be a good farmer. Although he had the personality of an angry boar, the man usually kept to himself. "Very well, ye can have an additional acre."

The man's face brightened. "Thank ye, Laird, Thank ye." He gave Alexander a slight bow and hurried away to speak to the scribe.

The rest of the day went by quickly until it was last meal. Alexander was exhausted, the candlelight in the great room making his eyelids heavy. He scanned the room and noticed that Nala wasn't at the table with his mother and wondered if perhaps she felt poorly.

Just as the meal was ending, the guard leaders came to where he sat. Hendry spoke for them. "Laird, ye asked us to be here to discuss work shifts and rotation with the guards returning to Uist."

He'd forgotten about it. He motioned to a nearby maid. "Bring mead to my study and see about something sweet for me." The woman hurried away as Alexander stood and walked with his men to the study ignoring the call from his body to go to bed.

THE FOLLOWING MORNING, Alexander woke feeling refreshed. He'd slept in late, which annoyed him, but he was glad for the rest. Once he washed up and dressed, he went down the stairs to find food to break his fast.

Somehow upon waking and realizing Nala was the first

thing on his mind, he finally understood how deep his feelings were for her. As soon as possible, he'd find Nala and clear things up and declare himself.

In a way he wasn't sure it was love. The word was startling, but he'd never felt so strongly for a woman before, so he supposed it was.

The great room was surprisingly empty except for a trio of people sitting at a table, making him realize that he did indeed sleep in longer than usual. As he neared the hearth, he noticed his mother and Ainslie, heads together whispering about something. Nala was not with them, and he wondered if she'd gone outside or perhaps returned to her bedchamber after first meal.

He walked to the women and cleared his throat. Both jumped. His mother looked at him and gave him a tight smile.

"Ye must have been very tired to have slept in so late." There was something about her, a sort of unease.

He looked from her to Ainslie, who looked just as bothered as his mother. "Is something wrong?"

"Of course not, nothing of importance," his mother replied not looking at him. "I will alert Cook to bring ye food. People will soon arrive seeking an audience." She got up and hurried away.

Narrowing his gaze at Ainslie, he noted she paled under his scrutiny. "Is something wrong with ye? Yer…"—he looked to her midsection—"Is it the bairn?"

"All is well." She patted her stomach, her lips curving. "It is normal for me to feel a bit unsteady in the mornings. Yer mother assures me it will pass."

Glad it was nothing more than Ainslie feeling a bit poorly,

he patted her shoulder and went to a nearby table where Cynden and Knox sat with the constable from the village.

Knox looked to him when Alexander sat. "Constable Macbean came to tell us what happened after we left yesterday."

The constable nodded. "All is well, Laird. The couple went home and apparently Cormac remained at the tavern until he had to be carried home. He was a sobbing mess, the poor lad."

Alexander shook his head. "Do ye think he'll cause more trouble?"

"Nae today, I bet his head is heavy from the drink," Cynden said with a smirk. "I feel badly for him, but naught to be done about things now."

"Aye," the constable agreed. "Cormac is nae a violent man. He will brood for a bit, but soon will be over it, I am sure."

Food was brought and placed before him, the thinly sliced meat and boiled potatoes with mashed peas were a perfect meal for a busy day of seeing to the clan.

THE LAST MAN finally came forward to speak and Alexander was glad for it. It was late afternoon, and he grew tired, wanting to go outside for fresh air. He planned to spar with the guards and perhaps ride out to visit an older farmer and his wife. They'd been on his mind since hearing the wife was gravely ill.

The man looked to him, he had a bruise on his right cheek and a knot on his forehead. He let out a long sigh whilst fidgeting with a dirty hat. "Laird, I beg yer help with my issue. My wife is gone with our bairns. Says she cannae live with me if I continue to go to the tavern. I did plan to stop, but she left anyway."

"Where did she go, Fergus?" Alexander asked studying the forlorn man.

"To her sister's cottage. I tried to visit, but they threw rocks at me and would nae let me near."

Alexander pressed his lips together, not sure if he felt badly for the man or wanted to laugh at the picture in his mind.

He looked to Cynden who shrugged and then Knox who shook his head. Neither were much help. "I say ye go home and clean yer house. Ensure yer sheep are taken care of and the garden kept up. Stay away from the tavern. Since they nae allow ye near, send a lad over to tell her ye are awaiting her return. Then wait."

The man gave him a confused look. "Can ye nae go and order her to return home?"

"Will ye stay away from the tavern? If nae, then she will leave again. I cannae force her to put up with yer antics."

Fergus' shoulders drooped. "Vera well, Laird. I will do as ye say."

"Return in a sennight and inform me of what happens," Alexander said and motioned to the scribe. "Remind me."

"Let us go spar," he said to Cynden and Knox. "I require fresh air."

He rose and went to find his sword, Cynden came alongside. "Did ye notice someone is nae here?"

"Do ye mean the council? I dinnae expect them for two days."

When Cynden gave him a pointed look, he stopped in his tracks. "Do ye mean Nala?"

"Aye, she left, yesterday. Mother said she came to her and said she needed to go home. Said she seemed cross."

"Did ye see her?"

"Nae. It was when ye and I were outside talking." Cynden's eyes widened. "Do ye think she heard us?"

"The rustling…" Alexander let out a long breath to keep his temper in check. "Why wait to tell me? Ye should have woken me as soon as ye found out."

His brother nodded. "I was going to, but we ken where she is and perhaps Nala requires some time to calm down. Mother said she was furious about something."

If not for the fact his chest tightened and stomach dropped, he would have hit Cynden. Alexander closed his eyes. "I will go find her."

"I can come…"

"Nae," Alexander interrupted him. "I will go alone."

Cynden lifted both hands in surrender. "Ye best tread lightly. The lass is a fiery one."

CHAPTER SEVENTEEN

Nala stood in the middle of her bedchamber. The tangle of emotions didn't allow her to sit still, much less rest.

After spending time the night before trying to explain to her parents that she didn't wish to remain at the keep any longer and that any search for a compatible husband was a useless quest, they'd remained oddly quiet.

The entire time her parents had exchanged silent messages, looking at each other as if they knew something she didn't. It annoyed her when neither seemed particularly upset.

When she'd excused herself to go rest, they'd both kissed her and wished her a good night, neither seeming particularly bothered by her distress.

Their lack of reaction had made Nala angrier than she already was. Why did no one take her feelings into consideration?

Of course there was the fact that she'd not been able to fully explain why she'd left as it would mean divulging the night with Alexander.

Her father would insist they travel to the keep immediately and then demand Alexander marry her. Which was the reason she'd left the keep in the first place. She didn't want him to feel obligated to do something he didn't wish to.

Overhearing Alexander confiding to his brother that he

felt forced to marry her had cut her deeply. At that moment, she'd realized she wanted more from him than he would ever be willing to give. It would be a heartbreaking quest to marry someone whose heart did not belong to her.

That he'd seemed resigned and his brother having to comfort him had almost crippled her. She'd had to dash away before hearing more as it would have certainly shattered her heart.

All night she'd tossed and turned unable to sleep as the words she'd heard repeated in her head. Now she could barely remember what exactly was said, had he said he'd marry her out of duty? Or had he said he was forced to because of what had occurred between them?

Either way, she'd never marry him when he would only do so out of duty.

Never would she marry Alexander knowing his feelings were not as deep. After all, it was not his fault. A person can't help how they felt about another.

She went to the mirror and peered at her reflection. It was quite obvious she'd not slept well, her eyes were puffy and red. For the first time in her life, she'd cried over a man. How silly was she?

"Nala?" her mother called from the other side of the door. "Are ye up and dressed?"

"I am."

The door opened and her mother came in. Dressed casually in her favorite shade, a mossy green, her mother looked beautiful.

She came to her and enfolded Nala in her arms. "My girl. All will be well, ye will see. Dinnae fret. Come downstairs."

Nala hugged her mother close. "I will," Nala said fighting tears. "Let me just brush my hair."

It was a quick moment to pull her hair up and pin it in place. Satisfied that she looked presentable enough, she went down to find her parents.

The front room was empty, so she peered in the kitchen where Cook was preparing a tray of food. The woman gave her a warm smile. "Yer mother is in the garden. She asked that ye go to the parlor."

Obviously, the parlor would be where they'd discuss her options. Her mother would suggest she marry a Grant, or perhaps someone else and she would have to argue against it. After the night with Alexander, she couldn't imagine having to bear another man's touch. At least not for some time. She needed time to heal.

She went toward the parlor, in her mind prepared for the conversation that would come. Letting out a sigh, Nala considered that life alone in the house wouldn't be so bad. Perhaps her brother and his wife—when he married—would come to live there and she'd have future nephews and nieces to care for.

Upon entering the parlor, she took a breath and lifted her gaze. In the room stood Alexander. Dressed in riding clothes, a tunic, breeches, and tall boots, looking every inch a warrior. His hair had been shorn short, which accentuated his angular features, strong jawline, and slashes for eyebrows.

He watched her without speaking, waiting for Nala to say something, but words eluded her. Instead she continued to study him, from the wide expanse of his shoulders to his broad chest, trim waist, and powerful legs.

"Nala. Why did ye leave?" He watched her closely as if he had the ability to tell if what she said was truth.

Nala let out a breath and managed what she hoped was a bland expression. "I felt it was time to return home. My being at the keep has been an utter waste of time."

"Do ye truly believe that?" There was something in the way he looked at her. Was it hurt? No, he didn't care that much. She'd heard what she'd heard.

Nodding, she met his gaze. "I mean as far as finding myself a husband. I can find one here just as well. There is nae need for yer family to continue to host me."

"Is what happened between us the reason for ye leaving?"

The question caused her cheeks to heat, so Nala turned away. "Aye, a bit. Not a regret, just that I would never wish ye to think I hoped to trap ye into marriage. I dinnae wish to be married to someone who does it out of obligation or duty."

Alexander neared. She could hear his breathing just behind her and for a moment she closed her eyes. When she turned, he was much too close, but taking a step back would show weakness, which she was too stubborn to show. "I am well, Alexander. There was nae need for ye to come."

"What if I am not?" His eyes took her in, lingering on her lips. "What if I said that I want ye there… with me?"

She flattened her hand on the wide expanse of his chest. "Ye dinnae have to say such things. I ken how ye really feel. I admire yer sense of duty. Ken that I would never hold ye to do what ye consider to be yer obligation. I will find a husband when I am ready and I'm sure it could be soon."

"Is that so?" he asked, his right eyebrow arching. "So ye have a man in mind already?"

Of course she didn't. Nala tried to come up with something to say. Finally she gave up and glared up at him. "Alexander, there is nae reason for ye to be here. We are and will always be friends."

For a long moment, he looked down at her with an unreadable expression. Perhaps annoyance.

He took her by the shoulders and leaned down until their noses almost touched. "When ye eavesdrop, stay long enough to hear the entire conversation. Then perhaps ye would have heard that the reason I was so confused was because I've never been in love before. I believe that I love ye Nala and it scares me. Nae it terrifies me. Ye have the power to destroy me, and I am nae sure how to feel about it."

A combination of reactions were uncontrollable. Nala's mouth fell open, she gasped, and her eyes went so wide it almost hurt.

"Ye… love… me?" Her heart leaped with joy. At the same time, she wanted to run from the room and hide. The emotions that coursed through her were like nothing she'd ever experienced before.

"Aye, I do Nala. I love ye more than life itself. I cannae bare to be away from ye." Alexander pressed his lips against hers and she immediately threw her arms around his neck and kissed him back with all her might.

When he broke the kiss and looked at her, she could see the truth of his declaration.

"I understand that yer feelings may not be as strong," Alexander began but stopped when she put her fingers to his lips.

A smile curved her lips. "I am in love with ye. I ached physically when I heard ye say marriage to me would be a duty."

"It is nae a duty," Alexander said wrapping his arms around her and lifting her off her feet. "It will be all pleasure, I assure ye."

"P︎︎︎ᴜᴛ ᴍʏ ᴅᴀᴜɢʜᴛᴇʀ down before ye drop her." Her father's firm command jolted Nala, and upon Alexander lowering her to the floor, she pushed away.

Her parents stood in the doorway. Her mother had an amused expression, her eyes twinkling with delight and her father attempted to look stern, but the slight curve of his mouth gave away his true feelings. Both were delighted by the turn of events.

Nala couldn't get her mind to settle. Was it truly possible that Alexander loved her?

Her father poured whiskey for him and Alexander, honeyed mead for Nala and her mother, and then motioned for everyone to sit.

Alexander calmly relayed to her parents that he'd fallen in love with Nala and wished to ask for her hand in marriage.

When Nala huffed, he slid a look to her. "If yer daughter accepts me, I wish to ken if ye are in agreeance," he clarified.

"Of course we agree," her mother exclaimed, not giving her father a chance to speak. "The lass is already feeling strongly for ye. I can tell by her ramblings last night."

"Ma!" Nala cried out. "Ye dinnae have to tell him everything."

Her mother waved her protests away and smiled at Alexander. "It would be wonderful to be part of the Ross family."

"Ye have my permission and blessing," her father said and

slid a look to her. The warmth of his expression made Nala swallow. Oh, how she loved her gentle father.

Nala's mother motioned to Alexander. "It is a beautiful day. Both of ye, go out to the garden so ye can have a proper talk."

Walking out ahead of Alexander, Nala wanted to be elated and happy, but instead she felt jittery and nervous. She wished with all her might to hear everything he'd said again. At that moment it was like a dream.

On a table in the garden was a platter of food. Nala shook her head. Obviously even the cook was in the plot to get her married off.

She turned to Alexander. "Why did ye cut yer hair?"

"I didnae mean to. But was eager to come here and cut one side shorter than the other. Mother tried to fix it and gave up." He raked a hand through the longer strands in the front. "Do ye like it?" His smile was enchanting.

"Aye, I do. Ye look very different. I prefer it longer because it hides a bit more of yer bonny face."

"Ye wish to keep my face hidden then?"

Nala rolled her eyes. "I didnae say that. But it will help keep women's eyes from lingering."

"Ye are trying to distract the conversation. I want ye to agree to marry me." Alexander reached for her hand.

"I-I cannae think straight. I heard clearly that ye felt it was a duty."

Alexander closed the distance between them and lifted her face. His eyes bore into hers. "Ken this my Nala. Ye are the only woman I want in my bed from now on. I cannae bear the thought of ye with another. I may nae ken exactly what love is, but I think it has to be this."

Searching his eyes, she could see only sincerity.

"Tell me aye, Nala. Marry me. Be my wife."

She couldn't deny him. No matter the reasons, he was her weakness. Nala let out a shaky breath. "Ye overwhelm my senses, ye stubborn Scot" She lifted to her toes and pressed a soft kiss to his lips. "I will marry ye Alexander Ross. Ye best prove it is nae a bother or I will shoot ye with my bow and arrow."

Alexander laughed and once again lifted her off her feet. This time he turned in a circle making her giggle.

"I will prove to ye over and over, that ye are the only woman for me."

Nala wrapped her arms around his neck and melted against him. "I ken what love is."

"Do ye?"

"Aye. It is the feeling of coming home and never wanting to leave."

THE WEDDING PREPARATIONS kept everyone busy and to Nala's delight, her mother and Lady Ross were too preoccupied to pay her much mind.

Just as were the men in her life, both Alexander and her father were busy with council business, making it easy to slip away unnoticed.

Her horse stood next to a winding creek as she leaned against the trunk of a tree, her gaze on a group of Ross warriors riding past.

One of the men turned to scan the area, his senses honed by years of experience. Nala wanted to giggle when he looked in her direction but didn't see her. The pounding of her heart made it difficult to breathe when he nudged another warrior and said something.

They exchanged a few more words, both looking around for just a bit before continuing forward.

Nala tensed. They had to have seen her horse. She looked down to ensure the beast was still there. It was gone.

The beast was well trained and had never once wandered away. She wasn't high enough in the tree to see far, but scanning the area, she couldn't see the horse. It didn't help that the sun was setting casting long dark shadows through the trees. Her horse blended perfectly with the hues.

Climbing down, she landed softly on the ground and hissed out the horse's name.

"Shadow."

"Shadow," she called out a bit louder.

Annoyed at the beast, she stomped forward toward the creek. The horse was probably drinking water and then fallen asleep.

She found it just a few moments later, next to another horse and Alexander, who held its reins.

It was too late to hide her bow and quiver, so she lifted her chin and walked up to him. "Ye should nae take someone's horse without their permission."

His deep green eyes met hers. "And someone's betrothed should nae run off without telling anyone, just in case they…"—he looked up—"fall out of a tree."

Despite knowing he was right, she worried he'd forbid her

outings. In truth, she'd not asked how he felt about it.

"I should have."

Seeming to read her thoughts, Alexander tipped her chin up with his finger. "I am aware ye require more freedoms than most women I ken. I would never change that about ye. However, as a laird's wife, we will have to discuss a compromise. Perhaps ye can foster young ones and teach them what ye ken."

Nala swallowed unable to believe how understanding he was being. "That is nae a bad idea."

He motioned to the area. "Ye are close enough to the keep, this area can be set apart for just that."

Unable to keep from it, she threw herself against him, her arms around his waist. "I truly love ye, Alexander Ross. Ye are to be the best husband ever."

He kissed her softly, then touched his forehead to hers. "Ye may not think that at all times. Especially when I tell ye that yer days as a rescuer are over. I will nae allow ye to put yerself in danger like that again."

Nala almost protested, but then thought better of it. She would never be able to sit idly by, at the same time, if the need arose, she could always ask for forgiveness.

"Stop thinking," Alexander said lifting her into his arms and lowering her onto the soft grass. "I can think of a better way to pass the time."

EPILOGUE 1

2 months later

"Do ye find me bonny?" The lass gave Knox's ear a playful nip, her heated breath fanning over it.

"Of course I do. Why else would I be here?" He'd tupped the lass before. She was without complications, never demanding anything from him. Knox found it best not to ponder too much on why she didn't seem to mind if he didn't call on her regularly.

"What makes ye think I will give ye what ye want?" She leaned back to meet his gaze, her eyes twinkling with mischief.

Knox smiled. "I dinnae ken for sure. Ye may nae." Just as he was about to kiss her, the breaking of a branch sounded. The lass leaned forward, eyes closed, with expectation, but Knox was distracted.

It would be disgraceful to be caught or attacked whilst unawares under a woman's skirts.

"Wait here," he whispered. "If ye hear fighting run home."

Wide-eyed, the lass silently nodded.

Despite the fact it could be no more than a deer, or someone out walking, Knox crept in the direction of the sound. There was no one in sight. He scanned the surrounding area and then studied the ground. He was known for his tracking abilities, expertly able to follow the path of whomever he sought.

The broken branch was just ahead on the path. Interesting, Whatever direction the person or beast went was hard to tell. It seemed as if they moved away from the way leaves on one bush were brushed.

Walking around a tree, he bent just in time to avoid being whacked by a long branch. The crunch of the wood against the tree's bark made a loud sound. Before he could say anything, the branch swung again, its wielder letting out a loud screech. This time he jumped back to avoid being hit.

The wee branch wielding woman was no match for Knox. He waited for the next swing, grabbed the branch, and gave it a strong tug. She released it as she tumbled forward to land on her stomach on the ground.

"Are ye daft?" he yelled, yanking the woman up by an arm. "What are ye doing in the woods alone Sencha?"

She looked a proper mess. Skirts torn. Half her hair had fallen over her face. Somehow, she remained fetching even in that state.

"Let me go!" She tried to pull away, whilst sweeping hair away from her flushed face. Her chest lifted and lowered, harsh breaths exploding.

When she tried to kick him, Knox whirled her around and pulled her against his chest. "Sencha stop."

All at once she stopped struggling and turned her head to look up at him. The bright blue eyes took him in.

"What are ye doing here?" Sencha asked.

She smelled of lavender and nature, the delicate figure fit perfectly between his arms and Knox was reluctant to release her.

"I will let ye go if ye promise not to try to hit me again." He purposely held her tighter, not as a warning, but because he'd always wondered what it would feel like to have the fiery lass in his arms.

"I will be still. I thought ye were one of the attackers and meant to kill me."

After one last inhalation of her hair, Knox released her, and she spun to look up at him. "Knox, I didnae ken it was ye. Are ye here alone? I thought to have heard more than one voice."

The way she tilted her heart-shaped face as she studied him made him want to lie. He glanced over his shoulder to the area where he'd been with the other lass. She was gone. Had probably fled when she heard the tussling.

"I am alone," he replied, not a lie, per se. "And ye, what are ye doing?"

"Looking for Blossom, my wee dog. She ran off earlier." She glanced around. "She's probably hightailed it home if she heard us."

He studied her torn skirts and messy hair. "What happened to ye?"

Brows lowered, she looked down at her dress. "It is nae easy to traipse about the woods in skirts. Branches reach out and snag everything, my clothes, my hair…" She motioned to her head.

Knox nodded. "It is best ye return home. I will walk ye back. Dogs are smart and return home when it is time to eat. Dinnae worry yerself."

Sencha didn't look convinced. She looked away from him, a frown on her features, seeming to consider whether or not to continue her search. Then she studied him. "I am surprised ye are nae in the village chasing after women. Where's yer horse?"

"I return from visiting my parents. Ye ken they live near ye." He pointed to the right. "My steed is there."

Her eyes narrowed in thought, looking from the horse to him. "Why is he tethered and ye are walking about the woods?"

The lass was smart. He had to acknowledge that a man involved with her would have to be someone who was either quick on his feet, or totally honest at all times.

"I walked into the woods to find relief and was about to do just that when I heard ye step on a branch." Again not a lie.

"Oh,"—she blushed—"I see." She made shooing motions with her hands. "Well go on then. I will look a bit more for Blossom then go home."

Now he had to pretend to relieve himself. Knox let out a breath. "I will walk ye about. Ye should nae be about on yer own. Even with the branch, which ye did wield well, harm can come to ye."

Knox held up a hand. "Wait here."

He went to where his horse was, nibbling on the grass, seeming oblivious to what occurred. Taking the reins, he guided the huge warhorse to where Sencha awaited.

It was the first time he'd had the opportunity to spend time alone with the pretty lass. Sencha was one of the few women who seemed immune to his charms. Each time he'd tried to get her attention, she'd rebuffed him. That he knew of, no one had yet to court the flame haired beauty. Not for lack of trying, but because she pushed away every attempt at conquest.

"We have known each other for a long time," Knox said by way of conversation. It was time to try a new tactic with her and perhaps friendship could lead to more.

"Aye, since we were wee," she replied giving him a sideways glance. "Ye are older, so we were nae friends."

His smile was careful, controlled. "We can be friends now."

"Aye, I suppose."

"My heart melts from yer enthusiasm," he teased.

The words elicited a laugh, a throaty sound. "I dinnae mean to sound less than enthusiastic, it is just that I am truly worried. My Blossom is wee and alone. What if something gets her?"

Knox whistled several times, whilst Sencha called out the dog's name. They continued in a wavy pattern heading back towards where Sencha lived. Knox was sure the dog was home by now, but he didn't wish to end the time he spent with the lass.

"Ye've had the dog for long?"

Sencha nodded. "Aye, for years. She is getting old. Cannae see well."

As they walked down the last patch of woods, Sencha looked as if she were about to cry. "Where can she be?" Her shiny eyes lifted to his. "Do ye really think she went home?"

It took all his willpower not to pull her close and comfort her. Instead he acted as a friend would and placed a hand on her slight shoulder. "Let us go and find out. If she is nae at yer house, I will ride back out and search for her."

"Thank ye, I do appreciate it." To his surprise, she threw her arms around his waist and hugged him. It wasn't a long hug and certainly not meant to be in any way flirty, but it made Knox feel as if he'd won first place in a competition.

The dog was nowhere to be found and as they neared Sencha's house, Knox noted a dog did not trot out to greet Sencha. She was just as disheartened. "It seems she is nae here."

Just then the door opened and a woman, whom he recognized as Sencha's mother, stepped out. She wore a serviceable, but well-tailored dress, and her hair was styled in a fashion that told she'd had help from a maid. Sencha's family-owned lands were connected to Ross lands. Her family was not as wealthy as Nala's, but they were able to hire farmhands and servants to care for the large house.

"I was worried. Where have ye been?" the woman called out as they neared. "Knox," she acknowledged him.

Sencha let out a shaky breath. "Searching for Blossom. I cannae find her."

Shaking her head, her mother's gaze scanned from Sencha's disheveled hair to her torn skirts. "Lass, ye look a fright. The dog returned a long while ago and is sleeping by the hearth. I was about to send someone out to search for ye."

"Oh," Sencha exclaimed, hands clutched over her chest. "I was so worried." She gave Knox an apologetic look. "Thank ye for helping me."

Her mother eyed Knox, seeming to see through him. "I am grateful she came upon ye. This foolish lass went traipsing in the woods alone. Anything could happen, Sencha," she finished pinning her daughter with a look.

The older woman once again turned her attention to Knox. "Come in for some cold ale before ye continue wherever it is ye were heading."

"I best not," Knox replied, not liking the way the woman

watched him. It was as if she knew how strongly he was attracted to her daughter. "I am expected at the keep."

As he rode away, he glanced over his shoulder toward the house and a smile played on his lips. Perhaps he'd finally made headway towards getting to know Sencha. Then, with a bit of patience, he would use all his well-honed skills to seduce the lass.

Seduce. The word didn't give him the thrill of the hunt that it would normally. Something in his gut told him that if he ever accomplished this particular goal, there would be no going back. Sencha was not a one-time woman, but the kind of woman that bespelled a man to remain forever. For whatever reason, the idea of it didn't terrify him.

That changed his decision. Perhaps it was best to use all means possible to stay far away from her.

LIPS PRESSING AGAINST his then moving to his jawline sent heat through him. The comfort of the moment was surreal. He didn't want to wake from this wonderful dream. His body was coming to life. Soft hands slid up and down his chest. The plush lips continued to press kisses, making him turn his face toward her.

He became hard as stone. His body demanding more than the feathery touches. More than the light kisses.

When Alexander finally managed to open his eyes, he looked directly at the most beautiful creature he'd ever known. Ringlets surrounded a breathtaking face, half-closed eyes met his as kissable lips curved into a seductive soft smile.

"Nala." His voice was hoarse from sleep, but it conveyed the message because her hand continued a path downward past his stomach, then her thin fingers wrapped around his hardness.

At the touch, all air left his lungs. When her grip caressed from the tip to the base of his shaft, a moan escaped from his lips.

"Take me," he demanded, praying she would. "I need to be in ye."

Nala's agreement sounded like a purr in his ear as she gave him one last kiss before climbing over him and straddling his midsection.

She was perfection. From the tussled dark curls and pert breasts to the slender waist and the flare of her hips above her powerful thighs.

Leaving a trail of fire, her eyes moved from his face to hesitate on his lips before moving past his stomach to his hard sex. "Ye do want me."

To his delight, she lifted up just high enough for him to enter her. Unable to withstand another moment without taking her, Alexander grasped her hips to help her, and himself. He needed to set the pace or else he'd spill immediately.

She shifted so that they were aligned and slowly lowered. Taking him in, inch by inch. All the while, her eyes never leaving his.

Upon taking him fully, both let out a groan of satisfaction and she threw her head back, her already snug sex tightening around him.

Lovemaking with his wife was nothing like it was with any

other woman, Alexander had never known the act could be so intimate, so personal, and so satisfying all at once. Each motion with Nala was so much more enjoyable than entire interludes with other women.

Enjoying the view of her, he wanted nothing more than to watch as she lost control. Knowing what she liked, what overwhelmed her, he took each breast in hand and circled the taut peaks with the pads of his thumbs. She instantly reacted, letting out short breathy gasps.

Then to his delight, she leaned over him, the tips of her breast teasing his mouth until he took one in. Sucking first one and then the other hard. Loving the way she quivered around him in response.

"Alexander," she gasped out his name as she began lifting up until only his tip remained inside her. Then lowering and taking him fully. Time and again, she moved slowly. Deliberately. Tantalizing him. Knowing he would be unable to take it for much longer.

Barely able to keep his tenuous control, he pushed his head back onto the bedding, and closed his eyes, enjoying the feel of her lush curves, her tight sex, and her heated breaths fanning over his face.

"Nala." He breathed more than said her name, unsure what he wanted to say. Though it didn't matter because she chose that time to take his mouth as she began to ride him harder, faster.

She continued taking him, over and over, her body becoming slick from the exertion. He didn't want it to ever stop, but his reaction was becoming fevered, and he had to take over.

Alexander tightened his grip on her hips, taking her fully

by lifting his own, thrusting into her heat.

"Ah!" She began to shake as her first release assaulted her, and she pushed into him. Once she relaxed, he swiftly rolled her over and pulled her legs up and over his shoulders.

Nala let out a loud moan as he pushed in fully. Steadily driving deeply into her wet center. Suddenly, all control was lost, both of them thrashing, pushing for the other to find release.

The sound of their bodies colliding filled the room, fueling the fire that was raging inside him. Alexander drove over and over into her willing body, his release so eminent, he could barely breathe.

He came. It was as if his entire body shattered in the most satisfying way. He was aware that Nala was lost in her own wave of passion as she stiffened and then went slack. But he was too consumed by his own to do anything more than allow the waves to wash over him.

Collapsing over her, Alexander couldn't move. Nala's eyes were closed.

He had to move, was too heavy to lay atop her, but his bones felt like water.

"Alexander, I can't breathe," Nala said nudging him.

"Sorry." He managed to lower her legs, before collapsing beside her. Then he pulled her against him. They'd have to sleep for a bit longer before being able to head down to first meal.

Nala snuggled against him, and he kissed her temple. "I love ye with all my being, wife."

"I can scarcely believe I get to wake up to ye every morning. I love ye more than ye can imagine," Nala told him in a sleepy voice.

Her hand reached up to cup his jaw and they looked into each other's eyes. Nothing more needed to be said.

EPILOGUE 11

"WHERE'S YER HEAD?" Cynden pushed past Knox and pointed at the target. His arrow was lodged on the very edge. "Head in the clouds today cousin?"

Knox grunted trying his best to come up with a reason for his distraction.

Never would he admit thinking of a woman distracted him from target practice. In truth, he'd replayed the same scene every time.

Alexander's wife, Nala, had company. A beauty named Sencha MacTavish. Both women, at that very moment sat under a tree. Next to her was the idiot Hendry, doing his best to get their attention. Obviously it worked, because both Sencha and Nala threw their heads back and laughed.

"She is quite bonnie, but will never be for the likes of ye," Cynden commented, shaking his head. "Sencha is much to sensible to fall for yer ploys."

"I have nae interest in the lass. She is someone a man seeks for marriage." Knox made a show of shuddering. "Nae for me."

Cynden looked back toward where the woman now sat alone, Hendry on his way toward the keep. "That my friend, is true. Do nae forget it." When he turned his attention back to Knox there was a subtle warming in his gaze.

With a huff, Knox turned back toward the target and reached back for a new arrow. He closed his eyes and steadied his breath.

The subtle breeze carried not only the scent of freshly cut flowers, but Sencha's voice.

"That's enough for today," Knox said lowering his bow and stalking away, ignoring Cynden's knowing grin.

Read Knox's story in The Falcon!

About the Author

Enticing. Engaging. Romance.

USA Today Bestselling Author Hildie McQueen writes strong brooding alpha Highlanders who meet their match in feisty brave heroines. If you like stories with a mixture of passion, action, drama and humor, you will love Hildie's storytelling where love wins every single time!

A fan of all things pink, travel, and stationery, Hildie resides in eastern Georgia, USA, with her super-hero husband Kurt and three little yappy dogs.

Let's stay in touch, join my NEWSLETTER for free reads, previews of upcoming releases and news about my world!

Printed in Dunstable, United Kingdom